JAMILA GAVIN

EGMONT

This book is respectfully dedicated to Stephen Hawking. Grateful thanks to Robert Barr, Jean-Pierre Melot and Professor John Harries

First published in Great Britain 1996
Reissued 2003
by Egmont Books Limited
239 Kensington High Street, London W8 6SA

Text copyright © 1996 Jamila Gavin
Cover illustration copyright © 2003 Bob Lea

The moral rights of the author and illustrator have been asserted

ISBN 1 4052 0065 0

1 3 5 7 9 10 8 6 4 2

A CIP catalogue record for this title is available from the British Library

Typeset by Avon DataSet Ltd, Bidford on Avon
Printed and bound in Great Britain by the CPI Group

CONTENTS

1
FINDERS

Wherever you are the perspective can be a true one

The sand stretched and curved round into a blue, liquid haze. At first she thought there was only land and sea and sky, though sometimes she couldn't decide which was which. Sometimes she didn't know if she stood or swam or flew. It was as though she was slowly revolving – and moved – but without direction.

She wasn't sure how she came to be before the great egg-shaped life force. She wasn't aware of choosing to go towards it; things didn't work that way. She just knew that it was there, in a fixed spot in a space between earth, sea and sky, and that somehow she must communicate with it.

She had discovered that the only way to find direction, was to need it.

'I need to speak to you,' she heard herself say. So now she was tipping and turning as though strapped to a gyrotop and suddenly she was before the egg.

'I want to go back,' she said. She was sure her body had turned to tears.

'There is no back or forwards,' came the reply, though not in words. She heard it as a kind of humming, which rose and fell like the wind, and, somehow, she understood. 'There is no back, as in the past, and there is no forwards, as in the future; there is only creation and destruction and the bit in the middle,' the egg informed her.

Far out in the ocean, the whales were singing. She heard their high harmonies rising and falling and interweaving. Her mother had loved whales.

The shell of the egg had been a hard white – too bright to look at directly – but, as she listened to the singing whales, she heard her mother's voice trying to join in.

'Is there memory?' she asked.

'There is creation and destruction and the bit in-between,' repeated the egg, 'and there is re-creation – living it again. Some might call that memory.'

She felt a wave of triumph. A tiny glimmer of understanding and, with it, hope.

Suddenly everything was moving. She looked down at her feet, and the sand was rushing between her toes, carrying her away. Was the tide coming in, or was the land on which she stood sweeping her towards the sea? She let go of her reason again, and felt herself revolving once more. She called out to the egg. 'I need the bit in-between my creation and my destruction.'

The egg was glowing pink, orange, gold. The sea and sky merged with each other and turned aquamarine, iridescent and shimmering before disappearing into a night.

'Go with the wormholers,' she heard the egg whispering as it faded from sight.

2
THE BIT IN-BETWEEN

There is more to seeing than meets the eyeball

Norwood Russell Hanson

Chad stood staring at the kitchen shelf. His stepmother Angie had asked him to get the baking powder. It stood between the carton of ginger and the soy sauce. He saw it but, as his hand stretched out towards it, it vanished. He stared, stepped back and looked again.

'Hurry up, Chad,' cried Angie.

'I can't . . . see it,' he said.

'It's staring you in the face,' she exploded impatiently. 'Honestly, Chad, are you blind?' She turned rapidly to get it for herself. Her hand shot

4

towards the usual place on the shelf, then hesitated.

'See?' gloated Chad, triumphantly.

'If you had taken the trouble to look, you would have found it,' declared Angie scornfully, suddenly noticing the baking powder. It had found its way to the top shelf and was now standing between the tomato ketchup and the wine vinegar.

Chad's irritation set all his nerves on end and he muttered rudely under his breath. Normally, he would have been out with his mates on a Saturday afternoon, rambling along the canal or messing about in the shopping arcade, but today his grandparents were visiting. Well, they weren't really his grandparents, not in a blood-related way. They were *her* parents, and she wasn't his real mother. So he felt pretty cheesed off at having to stay around and play the dutiful grandson bit. Besides, he knew they disapproved of him. He could tell by their stupid remarks. They pretended they were jokes, and were usually accompanied by a titter or an over-familiar slap on the back, but he knew how critical they were of him – and, in the absence of his real mother, of the way she had brought him up.

'You're like a terrorist, with your hair cut short

like that!' Stepgrandfather had once guffawed, cuffing him on the side of his head.

'I'm surprised your mum lets you wear an earring,' commented Stepgrandmother. 'Do all your mates have their ears pierced? You look like one of those savages.'

Yes, that just about summed it up. They thought he was a savage and he knew they pitied their daughter for having to be a mother to him.

No one pitied him and the way he had had to put up with everything since his mother had packed up and left. Left his dad. Left him. He couldn't understand it. He didn't remember them quarrelling, not like some parents he knew. Whenever he asked why, his dad just shrugged. There was her note, which he read every six months or so to try and understand. *It's best for you that I've gone,* she had written. *I need to sort myself out. I'm going to travel round the world, find out who I am and then I'll come back a better person.*

Trouble was, she never came back. She got as far as Thailand and met some backpacker from New Zealand and went on to live with him. She wrote to Chad and said she had 'found herself', and would he like to come out and live in New Zealand? But Chad, after he'd smashed up his room and had a good weep, said, 'No way!' and firmly tried to put her out of his mind.

Of course his dad got a divorce as soon as he could, and pretty quickly married Angie. And thus, Chad acquired not just a stepmother, but a stepsister too.

Chad remembered with a shudder the day he was introduced to them. At first glance, he wasn't sure which was mother and which was daughter. His dad hadn't helped. He had just said a little sheepishly, 'Chad, this is Angie and Natalie.'

As mother was trying to look younger and daughter was trying to look older, and as they were both the same height and wore the same sort of clothes and both clung to his father in a rather proprietorial sort of way, it wasn't surprising that Chad was a bit confused. It was only when one of them relinquished his father's arm and stepped forward to give him an awkward motherly hug, that he realised this was Angie.

Chad had refused to look them in the eye and grunted, 'Hiya,' inwardly deciding he would hate them forever.

'Hello, Chad! Tony – your dad – has told me so much about you!' Angie had enthused. 'It's wonderful to meet you at last. My, but you're quite the handsome one, isn't he, Nat?' She was overdoing it and her voice petered away with embarrassment, while Natalie giggled.

So Angie's family had to become his family too, as everyone tried to make things return to a normal home life. But Chad didn't feel normal. It felt like a big lie. He refused to call Angie 'Mum', so he called her Angie; and he refused to call her parents 'Grandpa and Grandma', because they weren't his real grandparents. They thought he was too young to call them Norman and Cynthia, so he called them mostly nothing or, if pushed, Mr and Mrs Bancroft.

As for Natalie, she had no such reservations. She wasn't going to call his father 'Tony', oh no! Chad knew her father had died, but didn't see that that gave her the right to take his father. The way she cooed 'Daddy', sat on his knee and fluttered her eyelashes at him, filled Chad with rage. Especially when, secretly, she could be sly and mean, pinchy and kicky with tongue sticking out when no one was looking. He dreamt of ways to get rid of her.

'Oh dear!' Angie was flapping, as she stirred her cake mixture. 'I know this isn't going to work!' She was always nervous when her parents visited. It was funny really and, if he'd let himself, Chad could have sympathised with her. It wasn't just him they got at. They were pretty critical of her too. They were that sort of people: always finding fault, no matter what.

'Now where's the vanilla essence?' Her hand went wavering along the shelves. 'Why isn't it in line with all the other bottles?' she wailed.

Chad was about to leave her to it, when suddenly his eye caught a glimpse of the little brown bottle of vanilla essence. It was standing between the carton of arrowroot and the cinnamon powder. He glimpsed it out of the corner of his eye, and was about to point it out to her, when he had the strangest impression of it sliding away behind a packet of cornflour. His eye travelled along the shelf and he had a sensation of himself getting smaller and smaller, and the chutneys, pickles, bottles and cartons on the shelf rising up as gigantic as skyscrapers till the shelves became a veritable skyline. They rose higher and higher, and the spaces in-between were like deep shadowy chasms. He saw a brief flicker like a match suddenly lit, then extinguished and he thought he saw the little bottle passing behind the tomato ketchup.

'Chad! Chad?' He heard the alarm in Angie's voice, as Chad found himself lying flat on the floor.

He quite enjoyed the fuss they made of him. Angie insisted he stay in bed for the rest of the day, which meant he missed the wretched visit of the grandparents. He pretended to be asleep when they came upstairs to say hello. And on Monday morning, instead of going to school, Angie took him to the doctor. But all agreed it was nothing serious and Chad never mentioned the odd experience he had had in the kitchen.

In fact, he had almost forgotten the incident, but one night he dreamt of the kitchen shelf. He dreamt he saw the jars and bottles getting taller and taller and he dreamt of the great chasm in-between. The dream became a nightmare and he felt himself being tugged, as if by a magnet, into a terrifying black gap between the mango chutney and the Branston pickle. He fought and struggled and grabbed at anything he could get hold of to save himself, and awoke to find he had fallen out of bed in a tangle of bedclothes.

His experience in the kitchen came back to him.

Had it been a dream too – some kind of day-dream? It had all seemed so real, yet it couldn't be.

He took his torch and lit his way downstairs to the kitchen. He shut the door and switched on the light and stood looking at the kitchen shelf, trying to remember in detail what had happened. Everything looked normal. He lifted the Branston pickle off the shelf, held it in his hands, shrugged and grinned at himself for his foolishness and put it back. It must have been something to do with his fainting. He helped himself to a large bowl of cereal and then went back to bed.

Some days later, he dropped a five pence piece. It rolled across the carpet to the edge where the floorboards were exposed. He bent down to pick it up, and immediately fell back in terror, as the gap between the floorboards seemed to open up like a giant canyon, plunging down into unfathomable darkness. The moment was swift, and when he looked again, everything was normal. Then the doorbell rang.

3
PROFESSOR TLINGIT

Why does the universe go to all the bother of existing?

Stephen Hawking

'Hello.' It was a curious body which stood before him; squat and grey and somehow sexless. Not even when the person spoke, could he be sure whether it was a male or female, the voice was high and airy and floating. 'My name is Professor Tlingit. I am a cosmographic geomorphologist investigating seismic disturbances and I wonder whether I might ask you a few questions?' The body who called itself Professor Tlingit pulled out a notebook and pencil.

'Er . . . if you want to speak to my parents, you'll

have to come back in an hour or so. They've gone shopping,' said Chad, not knowing what the person was talking about.

'No. You'll do,' said the professor, unconcerned. 'Now then. Have you noticed anything strange recently?'

'What do you mean by "strange"?' asked Chad warily.

'Well, for instance . . . any kind of disturbances? Is your house on firm ground? Have you suffered from any kind of subsidence? You know, cracks appearing in the walls, or a garden fence suddenly beginning to tilt or slide – or even fall down?'

'No . . .' said Chad thoughtfully. 'Not that I know about. My dad could tell you better, of course.'

'Do things go missing?' Professor Tlingit asked the question with a sideways look, like a bird sizing up its territory.

'How do you mean, missing?' asked Chad.

'I mean missing. Like things disappearing.'

'Our cat went missing for three days. We thought she'd gone for good, then she suddenly . . .'

'No, no, no!' The professor sounded annoyed and impatient. 'Not that kind of missing, silly boy.'

Chad felt himself blush with anger. 'Stupid git,' he muttered to himself. 'You'd better come back when my dad's home,' he said, sulkily withdrawing inside. 'Anyway, I'm not meant to talk to strangers. You could be a serial killer or something,' and he firmly shut the door.

'I'm sorry, Chad.' The professor's voice seemed to vibrate through the letterbox. 'It's my fault for not explaining properly. When I said missing, I meant things that are there one minute and gone the next You know, trivial things. Like you put down a pen, then when you go to pick it up again, it's gone. The sort of thing that happens all the time: those missing socks, single trainers, those books from the library. How many times have you said, "I'm sure I left it on this table"?

'I'll go now, Chad, but I'll come back another day when perhaps your mum and dad will be home. Meantime, here's my card. You can always contact me yourself if you think of anything.'

A strange round piece of luminous plastic appeared through the letterbox and dropped on the mat at Chad's feet. It was a hologram and, as he picked it up and the light from the window caught it, he realised there were all sorts of other squiggles and symbols on the card as well as the name *Professor O. Tlingit, Cosmographic Geomorphologist O.G.C.* which reflected in and out of his vision.

Impulsively, he flung open the door to take another look at the visitor – but there was no one there.

'Was this professor a male or a female?' asked Dad later, when Chad was trying to tell him about the strange visitor.

'I don't know. I couldn't decide,' answered Chad with a frown.

'Don't be daft. You must have been able to tell. You can see the difference between a man and a woman, can't you?' quipped Dad with a laugh.

Dad wasn't taking it seriously. His mind was on gathering his plans together for renovating a house for a client. There hadn't been much work around recently, and though he was trained as an architect, Chad's father had been forced to 'diversify', as he called it, by taking on all sorts of odd jobs like bits of carpentry or interior decorating. Then, suddenly, some rich young couple from London came down wanting to do up an old wreck of a barn on the outskirts of the town and Dad got the job.

'This is the breakthrough I've been waiting for,' he told the family breathlessly. 'If I do a good job, it could lead to more. There's nothing better than the grapevine for getting work. A good recommendation is better than five hundred pounds' worth of advertising,' and he had flung himself feverishly into working out designs and measurements and costing materials.

'What's a cosmographic geomorphologist anyway?' demanded Natalie, bursting in on the conversation which continued over supper.

'Someone who studies the earth, perhaps . . .' murmured Dad vaguely, drawing a line down the piece of graph paper he was working on.

'That's the geo bit. What about the cosmographic bit?' asked Chad.

'Oh, I don't know. Something to do with space, I suppose. Honestly, Chad. It sounds like someone was having you on. Now look, be a sport and leave me alone. I've got lots to do. We'll talk about it later,' grumbled Dad, reluctant to be interrupted.

'Cosmic is to do with space,' said Chad. 'So a cosmographic geomorphologist must be a . . .'

Chad searched for the right words.

'Someone who studies earth in space!' declared Natalie triumphantly. 'Was this person wearing a space helmet? Perhaps it was an alien. That's why you couldn't tell if it was a man or a woman,' and she broke out into peals of mocking laughter.

'Go on, scram!' yelled Dad. 'Can't you see I'm working? Go and chatter somewhere else.'

Natalie rushed off giggling. 'Just wait till I tell Amy that Chad met an alien.'

'Shut up!' growled Chad through clenched teeth. He was furious, because, though Natalie thought she was joking, she seemed to have hit the nail on the head with her impeccable logic, though he wasn't going to admit it to her – not in a million years.

Chad pounded up to his room, hearing Angie's inevitable wail following him up the stairs. 'Must you thud like an elephant every time? You ought to take ballet lessons.'

Chad reached for his dictionary. First, cosmic. Let's see what that means exactly, he thought. His finger traced down the page. Cosine . . . cosmetic . . . cosmetology . . . cosmic. His finger stopped and he read:

cosmic: *from the Greek word, kosmos, meaning order. Of the cosmos; relating to the universe as a whole. Cosmography: the scientific study of the structure of the universe.*

'Phew!' Chad whistled. He was impressed. He turned to G in the dictionary. G . . . g . . . geo. *Earth, of the earth*, read Chad. He continued down all the words with the start 'geo' – and finally came to:

geomorphology: *the science dealing with the nature and origin of the world's topographical features.*

'What?' exclaimed Chad out loud in confusion. 'Oh, I give up!' and he slammed shut the dictionary. Dad must be right. Someone was having him on. With a snort of exasperation, he switched on his computer and slotted in a game.

If only Natalie had known when to stop. But that was another of her annoying habits. She carried it on and on and on. 'Seen any more aliens, Chad?' she demanded without fail, every time they met.

Especially if she was in the company of Amy or her other friends. Then a general titter would go round. It seemed everyone knew about Chad's encounter with Professor Tlingit. No amount of threats from Chad could put a stop to it. She knew she was protected.

Then one day Chad, in a fury, grabbed her round the neck and shook her so hard he left thumbprints on her skin. It brought more than a ton of bricks down on his head from Dad and Angie. 'If you so much as lay a finger on her ever again, my lad, you'll regret the day you were born,' raged Dad. 'No son of mine is going to be known as a woman beater.'

Woman? thought Chad bitterly. She's nothing but a girl. Not even a girl – she's a scorpion.

Strangely, it was Angie who had more effect. After her initial outbreak of anger and distress, she sought him out in his bedroom, where he had been sent in disgrace, and spoke to him quietly and calmly. 'Look, Chad. I know things have been hard for you. You lost your mum and got lumbered with a stepmother and stepsister – and, if you've read the fairy-tales, we're all supposed to be evil and horrid, aren't we? But it works both ways, you know. Natalie lost a dad, and she's lumbered with a brother. I suppose it's worse for you, because she loves your dad as if he were her own father, whereas you don't love me. You don't even like me. So she doesn't need to feel jealous. But don't be too hard on her, Chad. Nat isn't as bad as you think. She's going through a stage, that's all. You know, girls ganging up together against boys and all that. But I wish you'd give her a chance. I wish you'd give me a chance.'

It was a nice speech. Chad took it in but he still saw it as a sign of weakness to let up, so instead of making any concessions or even apologising, he just turned his face to the wall and wouldn't speak. His heart was intent on revenge.

4 MISSING

Never say, 'I tried it once and it did not work'

Ernest Rutherford

It was about a week later. Chad was in his room messing about sorting some of his old toys. He dragged out the yellow, plastic bath which had been his as a baby, and was now overflowing with years of Lego and action dolls and bits of spaceships all jumbled up together. He hadn't played with this stuff for ages – not since he got his computer. Now, it brought back pleasurable memories. He'd been quite good at putting kits together. He tipped the bath so that a whole clatter of pieces tumbled on to the floor and, idly, he began to assemble a space buggy.

He was looking for the radar saucer which fitted to the roof of the buggy. He rummaged about with his fingers then, just at the moment he saw what he was looking for, that same crack in the floorboard opened up and the piece fell through. Chad lunged forward and slapped his hand over the space to try and retrieve it but, almost instantaneously, the chasm closed up to a crack so narrow that even a five pence piece wouldn't have slipped through.

He sat back on his haunches staring in disbelief, and he heard Professor Tlingit's words tumbling through the letterbox at him. 'When I say missing, I mean things that are here one minute and gone the next. If you think of anything, Chad, you can get in touch with me. Here's my card.'

Chad leapt up and went to his jeans lying in a crumpled heap by the bed. He felt in the back pocket and, with relief, drew out the strange, round, gleaming plastic card with the hologram.

As he looked at it, he remembered what his science teacher had once said at school. 'A scientist will only believe what he can test. "Show me the data," he will say, for no scientist will accept the result of one test. He wants to be able to repeat it and repeat it, and find out why and how, so that he can demonstrate the proof. Then maybe he can say it is true.'

Chad now took another piece of Lego. He took it over to the exact spot where he had lost the piece of radar, and placed it over the crack. He leapt back just in time, as the crack opened again and the piece disappeared.

'Flaming Nora!' he exclaimed, using an old expletive of his mother's. He was shaking. What if *he* had been over the crack. Would he have been swallowed up too?

Suddenly, his door burst open and in came Natalie. 'Have you taken my hair gel again,' she demanded accusingly. Her hair was all frizzed up and static from using the hairdryer.

'No, I haven't,' retorted Chad, just as rudely. 'Now, get out of my room.'

'Are you sure?' She didn't leave, but came further into the room, looking round. 'You're always taking it.'

He gulped hard, and stared. A terrible idea formed rapidly in his brain. Just a few more steps to the right, and Natalie would be standing over the crack.

'Is that it, there?' His voice trembled as he pointed to the shelf in the corner.

She turned her head without moving her feet. 'Where?' she asked.

'There – look! On that shelf. Can't you see it, blockhead?'

She took a step forward, then another. She was right over the crack. Chad saw it open – but it was so fast that, even though there was an instant's regret, and he would have called out a warning, it was all too late. Without a sound, Natalie was sucked down before the words had even formed in his mouth.

Chad stood like one utterly frozen, his breath still caught in his throat – unable to breathe in or breathe out. Finally, he collapsed to the floor on his knees and stretched out a hand towards the crack. It didn't open. He shuffled closer and put his palm right over, but the crack stayed firmly closed. He pressed his mouth to it. 'Nat? Natalie? Can you hear me? I'm sorry . . . I'm sorry, Nat . . . Oh God! What am I going to do?'

'Chad?' It was Angie. She stood in his open door looking at him with puzzlement. 'What are you doing? Have you lost something?'

Then, before he could answer, she said, 'Where's Natalie? She's left the bathroom in a terrible tip – wet towels all over the floor, shampoo bottles without their caps, hair in the plughole. It's too bad. Have you seen her?'

'N . . . no!' stammered Chad. 'No. I thought she went downstairs.'

Angie turned away, calling out, 'Natalie? Where are you? Come and tidy up the bathroom.'

There was a dreadful silence.

Chad moved. It was as if in a dream. His limbs floated in slow motion. His ears buzzed with strange tingling noises. He got downstairs, though he hardly remembered how. He went to the room below – it was the living room. No one was there, only Bossy, the cat. He looked up at the ceiling. It was magnolia white, clean and fresh and unmarked, just as his dad had left it after repainting it only about a month ago. Natalie's descent through the floorboards of his bedroom had not made its mark on the ceiling below. So where was she?

The phone rang. It was Amy for Natalie. Angie answered. 'No, Amy, she's vanished for the moment. She can't be far, but don't hang on. I'll tell her you called and get her to ring back.'

Chad returned to his room. He went to the spot where the crack in the floorboards had opened up. He felt sick inside. He could hear Angie calling her daughter through the house.

Answer her, Natalie, please answer her, begged Chad silently. It can't be true. She can't just vanish like that. Perhaps I'm going mad. With great deliberation, he took two steps and stood astride the crack, his body taut – braced for a fall. He shut his eyes. Nothing happened. With a shuddering sigh, he flung himself on to his bed and examined Professor Tlingit's plastic card.

'This is stupid!' Chad felt faint with panic. 'I can't read this. How am I supposed to make contact?' He gazed hopelessly at the squiggles which reflected on the shiny surface. Then suddenly he realised that the word 'formatted' came through when he twisted it towards the light. 'Of course!' He leapt towards his computer with a triumphant shout. This must be a computer disk. He switched on the machine and slotted it in. 'Beep beep bop beep beep bop bip.' After a number of swift and indecipherable sounds and symbols, the words 'Hello, Chad' appeared on the screen. Then came the question, 'Do you wish to consult Professor Tlingit? Y/N.' Chad tapped Y for 'Yes'. Another series of sounds and squiggles swept across the screen which suddenly all came together in a face. Professor Tlingit's face. The face spoke. 'Hello, Chad! I'm so glad you got in touch. Have you got something to tell me?'

Chad leapt back from the screen as if he had received an electric shock. This was a computer screen, not a television screen. How could he have a talking disk? Such things hadn't been invented yet, had they? And if they had, he didn't have the equipment for it.

Professor Tlingit spoke as if he could see Chad – could see what his reaction had been. He looked straight into his eyes and smiled reassuringly. 'It's all right, Chad. Don't be alarmed. This technology is unfamiliar to you, but quite harmless, I assure you. Think of it as a video-telephone. We are talking live. I can see you and you can see me. It was smart of you to realise that my calling card was a computer disk. It means that we can talk intelligently. I knew that if you were forced to find out about the disk and find me, it would be because you have something very important to tell me. Yes?'

Professor Tlingit's head cocked sideways again, as Chad remembered, like a bird – checking, waiting and listening. 'To speak to me, just press the key with the wave sign and I'll hear you.'

Chad almost crept back to the keyboard and looked for the key with the wave sign. It was there on the top line. He pressed it. 'Can you hear me?' he whispered.

'I hear you,' the professor reassured him. 'Has something gone missing?'

'Natalie, my stepsister. She . . . well . . .' and Chad rapidly told the professor about the piece of Lego, and then his experiment to see what would happen if Natalie stood over the crack. 'I didn't mean her to disappear completely. How am I going to tell Angie?' Suddenly, Chad was shaking and stammering and begging the professor to help him find her. 'Where is she? Who are you? What's it all about? I stood over the crack too, but it didn't open up under me. Why?'

'Hmmm . . . Why? How? When? Where? These are cosmic questions, Chad. This is what my job is all about. Look, I'm coming over. I need to see the exact spot where she vanished. I'll be with you in about half an hour. Just exit in the normal way.' The image on the screen fuzzed and went to blank.

5
THE WORMHOLERS

Thou canst not stir a flower without troubling a star

Francis Thompson

She saw them appearing out of a mirage of sea and sky and sand, blowing in the wind. They seemed like a team of climbers, all roped together, threading their way along a narrow cliff path above her head. From that distance they were as small as ants, and she couldn't quite make them out.

Her heart filled with hope. Perhaps they could tell her how to get back – though she had already become confused about what 'back' meant. Back where?

She began to make her way towards them. But she realised that it wasn't just a question of putting one leg in front of the other, it was a question of focusing on the exact spot that she wanted to reach, and then her body responded.

She concentrated hard and felt herself being propelled along, faster faster. She began to see them more clearly, and felt anxiety. Her hesitation slowed her down. From a distance, they looked ant-sized, but the closer she got to them, the more they did indeed look like ants – yet also like worms. Their bodies were made up into three parts, but each part was segmented and could undulate. They had legs and arms which they sometimes used, but their bodies could also wriggle, extend and contract. Every now and then, the leader would toss out a coil of something rope-like, and they would abseil down to a lower ledge, one after the other, until finally they reached the bottom.

She was moving swiftly towards them again, curiosity giving her momentum, when suddenly she saw a hole appear in the ground before them. It was very small but, one by one, they were dropping down into it.

'Stop!' she found herself screaming. 'Wait for me! For God's sake, don't leave me!'

The last body had disappeared into the ground and the end of the rope was being hauled down, when she flung herself bodily forwards and grabbed the end of it. Like being caught in the centre of a vortex, she felt herself sucked in. It was fierce. It deprived her of breath, of sight and sound. She thought she might be dying. Then suddenly it was all over and they were all sitting in a long metallic corridor, she, the last one, clutching the cord tightly in her hands.

'Who are you?' The voices penetrated her brain, not in words, just in meaning.

'I'm lost. I want to go . . . back . . . I want . . .' Her body was crying all over.

'Lost . . . Lost . . .' They repeated the word as if to familiarise themselves with the sound.

'Which universe are you from?' they asked.

'Is there more than one?' she replied, and her eyes looked at the line of creatures before her. From a distance, they had all looked the same – ant-like, worm-like – but now, as she studied them, she saw a number of them were very different. Some, like herself, had arms and legs and moved like humans. Others, with fins and gills, looked more like water creatures than land creatures. Then others looked like nothing she had ever seen before – blobs of shifting light; grey shapes which curved and looped; loose collections of molecules which fluctuated like flocks of birds in flight.

'Yes, there are more than one. There are millions. As many specks of dust you see floating in a beam of sunlight, there are ten times more universes. They burst into life and die – some as swiftly as a bubble.'

'I don't know the name of my universe. I didn't know there was more than one. What has happened to me? Where am I?'

'You must have fallen down a wormhole – tumbled out through a hole in your universe and fallen into another, here with us,' she was told.

This information coiled round her brain like thin smoke. 'Where is here and who are you?' she finally asked.

'Here is now and us is we and we are . . . wormholers. We worm our way through from one universe to another, living our own kind of existence. We are joined by life forms such as you, Lost. They stay until they find a universe they like. Then they remain while the rest of us keep moving. We prefer a life of travelling. What will you do?'

'I want to go back,' she repeated. 'Back to wherever I was. Home.' Tendrils of fear thrust themselves through her stomach and her chest, squeezing on her lungs, tightening her throat, suffocating her from the inside out. 'I want to go home. Please help me!' she whimpered.

They ignored her cry, but someone extended a feeler and lifted the silver chain which hung round her neck. 'What is this symbol?' it asked, examining the pendant which was attached to the chain.

'N for Natalie,' she said without thinking. Then self-recognition swept through her. 'My name is Natalie. N is for Natalie!'

'N is for Natalie. Natalie Lost,' the voices told each other. 'You see, Natalie Lost, all creation is random. Your arrival here was an accident. Only a random accident can take you back – wherever back is. Will you travel with us?' They began to move again, the antworms setting the pace and the others threading out the rope.

Natalie saw a stone, glittering hard as a diamond.

She picked it up and scraped on the hard surface *Natalie is lost*, then she grabbed the end of the rope and cried, 'Don't leave me. I'll go with you.'

6
ENTERTAINING SOPHIE

In the eternal silence within a crystal they may see
the happenings of the world outside

Goethe

'Where are your parents?' asked Professor Tlingit, as
Chad answered the door to the professor's knock.

'I don't have parents,' corrected Chad coldly. 'I
have a father. He's at work and my stepmother Angie
is out looking for Natalie her daughter. It's serious.
They'll call the police if Natalie doesn't turn up in an
hour or two.' Chad's voice choked up with guilt and
panic. 'I shouldn't ask you in. But I don't know what
to do. You can help me, can't you?' Chad stared at
him desperately.

The professor was strangely grey – the colour of dolphins. Chad caught a glimpse of hands protruding from the cuffs of a long grey coat. They seemed to be in skin-tight surgeon's gloves for they were smooth, nailless and unblemished. It was the same with the feet which were enclosed in tight, grey boots. Chad had avoided looking at the professor's face and making eye contact, but now, overwhelmed by anxiety, he needed to see some glimmer of hope.

No sooner did he look at the face, than he dropped his eyes with embarrassment. It was different. Not as he remembered when they first met. The head was large – too large, with lumps and bumps and odd growths of hair which looked more like seaweed straggling down. The face was taut, grey-skinned, with small shining round holes for eyes, two smaller holes for a nose and a mere slit for a mouth. Instead of ears, he thought he saw a set of three holes which were more like gills, but he couldn't be sure for they were within the shadow of the rim of a hat. Surely some terrible accident had deformed the face.

The professor hovered in the doorway, as if testing the ground. The huge size blocked out the daylight like a great grey rock. Chad hadn't remembered how big this person was, nor had he noticed the odd clicking noise. The sort of sound his grandad made with his false teeth.

'We will find Natalie, won't we?' Chad repeated.

The professor clicked and moved further into the house, looking around with great deliberation. Then he/she went into the living room below Chad's bedroom. Chad was about to explain this, but was dumbstruck by the way the professor seemed to float, rather like a balloon which has not yet been attached to a piece of string – airily bouncing. It was as though the briefcase he held was the only thing that prevented him/her floating to the ceiling.

The professor looked up at the pristine paintwork then down at the thick-ply wall-to-wall carpet. 'Hmmm.' The utterance was like the rippling of water.

'We will find her, won't we?' pleaded Chad again.

'Do you expect me to say, "Yes, Chad, of course we'll find her, Chad, don't worry about it," eh, Chad?' the professor's voice answered, sharp and high and without emotion. It reverberated round the walls. 'All I can tell you is, we have a problem and I am here to try and solve it. To give you false hope would be irresponsible and ridiculous. The reason I called the other day, making enquiries about seismic disturbances, was because I knew there were reports of wormhole sightings. And that means one thing – cosmic activity. Now, show me the exact spot where your sister vanished.'

'Stepsister,' corrected Chad, though he hardly knew why it mattered. He led him upstairs, aware that though he, Chad, thumped his way up to his bedroom making all the stairs creak, the professor seemed to glide upwards without a sound.

'Here.' Chad pointed to the crack in the floorboards. 'I was experimenting. I was told that three successful results make a scientific fact,' he explained. 'I was only trying to be scientific. One of my Lego pieces disappeared through the crack, which just seemed to open up and close again. I tried it again with another Lego piece. It disappeared. I tried it again – but with Natalie. Then she disappeared. You see, I didn't really believe my eyes. But she's gone. That's a fact, but I can't explain it. When I went to stand over the crack myself, nothing happened. What does it all mean?'

The professor opened the briefcase and drew out a piece of folded metal with a strange antenna on the end of it. The antenna opened out like an elongated music stand and extended across towards the fateful crack. It rotated dizzily in ever-increasing circles, making beeping sounds. 'My wormhole detector,' he muttered, by way of explanation.

'Wormhole?' Chad began to ask – then it happened again. That same sensation Chad had had before, of either his getting smaller or of the room's getting bigger. He looked at his chest of drawers. It was looming higher and higher; the books on his bookshelves towered over him like giant office blocks; his bed stretched away like an endless runway.

'Professor Tlingit?' he called out, but his voice seemed to fragment like broken glass.

'Incredible! Incredible!' The professor's voice splintered with excitement. 'I knew your house was on a cosmic swamp – right in the very middle of a creation cluster of baby universes.'

The room darkened, and there were small bursts of flickering lights, some as faint as fireflies. 'See! Do you see? Those are universes being born.' The professor had let go of the briefcase and was drifting across the room, holding the antenna like an ethereal fisherman.

Then the carpet in the middle of the room sagged into a small indentation, as if something sucked from below. It began to be drawn inwards and downwards, pulling everything with it. Chad hurled himself on to the bed. His desk and chair were swallowed up in a gulp. The drawers and wardrobe slid towards the centre. His baby bath with the Lego, his football boots and trainers – now his bed with him on it. He screamed. 'What have you done? What's happening? Oh help! Help!'

The professor was hovering and spiralling above his head as if caught in a twister. It was hard to tell, but Chad was sure that the slit of a mouth had widened into an ecstatic grin. The professor thrust the wormhole detector towards him. 'I am going down a wormhole to look for Natalie. If you want to come, hold on to the rod. If you don't, leap into the doorway. You'll be safe there.'

'I want to come!' yelled Chad, instinctively reaching out. He grasped the end of the rod, but had barely made contact when he was tugged violently by a magnetic force, so strong that he felt as powerless as a pin. Then he was tipped upside down, so that his feet scraped the ceiling, and he was looking headfirst down at the professor who was now exactly over the crack in the floor.

There was a great whooshing sound. The professor chortled, like a child ecstatically terrified at the top of a roller-coaster, and was sucked from view down the hole. On the other end of the rod, Chad was dragged down too but, before he reached the rim of the hole, it closed up and he slammed on to the floor, still clutching the rod.

For a while he lay gasping and winded, feeling the pain rush through his bruised knees and elbows. Even when his breath gradually returned, he couldn't bring himself to turn and face the reality of what had happened. Or was it reality? Had he had some kind of blackout again and dreamed it all? He rolled over slowly on to his back. He could see a smudged juddering mark where the rubber soles of his shoes had scraped across the ceiling. Filled with dread, he turned his head sideways and saw the gap where his desk and chair had been. The rest of his furniture surrounded him in the middle of the room like a barricade, and all that was left of his carpet was a thin thread trapped in the crack of the floorboard.

Downstairs, the telephone was ringing again. He heard Angie pick it up. She was breathless. 'Yes, darling . . . no, darling . . .' She was speaking to his father. 'Natalie's vanished. I don't understand it. One minute she was washing her hair and the next minute she was gone. I've just been all round the neighbourhood looking for her. I can't help wondering whether she and Chad had another fight. He looked very odd when I asked him if he'd seen her . . . yes, darling . . . no, darling . . . well, I suppose she could have gone out in a huff, but she's meant to be entertaining Sophie today. She'll probably turn up at teatime. Oh, Tony, it's fish pie for supper – your favourite. Yes. I love you too. Byeee . . .' and she made kissing noises down the line.

'Chad! Chad!' Angie was calling him. 'Can you come down a minute?' Slowly Chad uncoiled himself from the floor and got to his feet. A great fear swept over him. He kicked the rod away from him with repugnance and dashed to the door. He trembled on the threshold, remembering what Uncle Bob from California had told him. 'Make for the doorway, Chad. That's what you do if you're caught in an earthquake. Make for the doorway. That's where the structures of a building are at their strongest.'

It was on a threshold that Professor Tlingit had told him to go, if he didn't want to fall down the wormhole. But he couldn't stand in doorways for ever. He was overwhelmed with panic as those familiar floors, stretching all round him, now looked as dangerous as sinking sand. How could he ever again be sure that the ground beneath his feet was solid? How could he ever be sure that the next step he took would not plunge him down into some black hole? And where, oh where, was Natalie?

Angie ran halfway up the stairs and peered up at him through the banisters.

'Chad! Have you seen Natalie?' She caught a glimpse of his room. 'What on earth have you been doing to your room? It's in a shambles!'

'Just rearranging the furniture,' muttered Chad.

'Are you all right? Where's Natalie? Have you and she had another fight?'

'No!' came his automatic denial. 'I mean, yes!' He suddenly realised that 'yes' was the answer that would at least stall Angle for a bit while he thought out what to do and when to tell her. 'She rushed off in a mood,' which was, after all, true. 'She's probably gone to Amy's.'

'Well, she's too bad, going off like that without telling me,' grumbled Angie. 'I just hope she hasn't forgotten it's her day to entertain Sophie. I'd better ring Amy,' and she turned to descend the stairs.

'Er . . . no . . . I've just remembered. Not Amy . . . someone else . . . I can't remember who . . .' Chad cried desperately, for Amy had only just rung up, and she would soon confirm that Natalie wasn't with her.

'Sophie?' asked Angie.

'No. She didn't mention Sophie. Oh, I don't know. Perhaps she's run away. Yes, she could have. She's always threatening to.'

'I've never heard her say that – not ever!' gasped Angie in distress, and she looked up at him with silent accusation, as if to say, 'What have you done to my daughter to make her want to run away!'

'It's not my fault,' muttered Chad angrily. 'I didn't do anything to her.'

'Well, I think you'd better go over to Sophie's in case Nat has forgotten. If she's there, give me a ring and then you can carry on to David's house. If not, please stay with Sophie and entertain her for about

45

half an hour. Oh, and just call in on Amy on your way and see if Natalie's with her. If she is, tell her to go to Sophie's and ring me from there so that I know where she is, do you hear?'

'Yes, Angie.' Chad's voice was so full of despair that Angie's gaze focused on him sharply. 'Are you sure you're all right?' Her voice softened with concern. 'You look pale.'

Chad couldn't meet her eye. He looked down and shrugged. 'Yeah, I'm all right. Didn't I say I was?' he retorted rudely.

'See you later then,' she said stiffly and hurried away.

Sophie. Chad groaned. Sophie lived a few streets away. She was Chad's age but had been born with cerebral palsy and was as helpless as a baby. Sophie's mother, Carol Walcott, had been his mother's best friend and they had been greatly involved in organising a rota of people who would keep Sophie entertained and stimulated. The Walcotts had never given up hope that one day, by stimulating all possible parts of the brain, she would be able to learn to do something. Speak? Control her limbs? Something. They always believed that there was an intelligent, lovely person locked into an uncooperative body.

When Chad's mother left, Carol missed her terribly. 'What am I going to do without Lyn?' she had wailed.

Then after a while Angie came and soon she and Carol Walcott were friends too. Angie became really interested. She went on to the rota immediately and persuaded Natalie to be on it too.

Chad flatly refused at first when Angie tried to persuade him. 'Mum didn't make me,' he argued, and wouldn't budge until his father had a word with him. Then with very bad grace he muttered, 'Oh, all right,' agreeing to go on the occasions Natalie couldn't. Even though it only meant staying about an hour, Chad resented giving up his time and hated the way Angie made him feel like a selfish pig. 'Moral blackmail,' he grumbled. 'Entertaining Sophie is like playing with a cabbage. I don't know why you bother. She really doesn't notice.'

'Well, that's where you're wrong,' Angie had said indignantly. 'It's only her body which is useless. Her brain's perfect, I know it is.'

'How can you tell?' Chad had protested. 'She

can't speak. She can't tell you anything or show you anything. All she does is slobber.'

'I can tell by her eyes. I can tell by the way she watches. I can tell by the way she listens that she's understanding everything,' insisted Angie. 'There's a person like you imprisoned in her body, Chad. Can you imagine how lonely that must be? Try and be a friend.'

So Chad became a 'friend' occasionally, which mostly meant playing with toys in front of Sophie, who lolled in her wheelchair, her hands waving uncontrollably in the air, breaking into strange shrieks and grunts from time to time.

From his bedroom doorway, Chad stuck out a foot and tested the ground, then bolted downstairs and out into the street. For once, he was glad to go to Sophie's. Anything to get away from his terrible bedroom. Anything to get away from the awful fact that Natalie had disappeared down a black hole and that he didn't know if she would ever come back. Also, by doing one good deed, it helped him to stave off the feeling of being a murderer.

He jogged along the pavement, making sure that each footfall was on a square and not a crack. His whole being was squirming with unease. His brain was in a state of fuzz, like a badly tuned radio. He met people he knew but couldn't bring himself to look them in the eye. He came to Amy's gate but didn't go in. There was no point. He knew Natalie wasn't there. He turned the corner, crossed the road and arrived at Sophie's house.

It was evident immediately that there was something different about this household. There were no front steps, for instance, but a ramp along which a wheelchair could be pushed. Chad and his mates used to like that ramp in the days when they were into skateboarding. Sophie would sit in her wheelchair in the open door, all twitching and jerking, to watch the children hurtling down and doing their flips and jumps and turns – and sometimes falling. The Walcotts were sure she enjoyed watching, but Chad couldn't tell and didn't much care anyway.

He rang the bell. Sophie's mum opened the door.

'Hello, Mrs Walcott,' muttered Chad with lowered head.

'Oh, it's you, Chad! That's great. I was expecting Natalie. Can't she make it today?'

'Nope,' answered Chad shortly.

'Sophie's in her room. She's longing to show off her new acquisition.'

Chad snorted inwardly. Mrs Walcott always spoke like that – as if Sophie was normal, as if she had said, 'Ooh, Mum, I can't wait to show off my new whatever it was.' Chad was certain that all she had done was grunt and squeal, and that she didn't know the difference between a piece of Lego and a banana. What was the word they used for people who talked about animals as if they were human?

Chad went through to the back. They had converted a room for Sophie with French windows out on to the garden. Everywhere downstairs stairs was open-plan: no doors or steps, with one room giving way to another. Everywhere was wheelchair accessible and everything was at wheelchair height.

The music centre was playing a song when they entered Sophie's room. *Speed, bonnie boat, like a bird on the wing* . . . 'Sophie's favourite song,' smiled Mrs Walcott.

Chad hardly noticed. He had stopped dead and raised his eyebrows with interested surprise as he saw the 'new acquisition' fixed to Sophie's wheelchair before her on a special tray. 'Oh!'

'Yes, it finally came. Sophie's going to learn to use it. Do you realise what that means, Chad?' Mrs Walcott's voice trembled with excitement. 'If she can learn to use the computer, she'll be able to communicate. She'll be able to tell us what she wants and what she's thinking. It will be like being reborn, like being let out of a terrible prison. Angie says you're good on computers. Perhaps now Sophie's got one, you won't mind so much coming here and giving up part of your Saturday. You can play computer games – perhaps teach her!'

Chad blushed. Had it been so obvious that he minded coming to amuse Sophie? He looked over the new computer and felt a stab of envy. He hadn't seen one as advanced as that before. His own was positively antique compared to Sophie's. 'How will she ever be able to do anything with the computer?' asked Chad, stroking the machine with awe. 'She can't control her hands, can she?'

'No, but she can control her head. They are teaching her to use a tool which is strapped to her head. Isn't it amazing? All she needs is to be able to nod her head and direct the tool to the letter she wants – and the whole world will open up to her.

She'll be able to read and write and think and even draw pictures. But most of all, she'll be able to communicate with us and we with her!'

She turned off the song and went over to Sophie. She put her hands round her daughter's head. 'Darling,' she said softly, 'Chad's here to see you.'

Sophie's limbs began thrashing as they always did when she was excited. Mrs Walcott took her arms and held them down firmly, then she moved the wheelchair sideways to make room for Chad. Chad came up and stood where Sophie could see him.

'Hi, Sophie!' said Chad in the jolly voice he had perfected over the years he had been visiting her. He had always felt that talking to Sophie was like talking into an answering machine. You tried to speak normally, as if someone was listening and understanding, but with no confidence that you would ever get a reply.

Sophie started twitching violently again and opened her mouth like a young fledgling demanding food. 'Aaah! Aaah! Aaah!'

Mrs Walcott said, 'I think Sophie wants to try and communicate with her headstick.'

Chad got out of the way as Mrs Walcott grasped

Sophie firmly and placed a band over her head and down on to her forehead. Then she angled it so that a long plastic tool could be aimed at the keyboard just by tipping the head forwards.

For a while, Sophie's body jerked so violently Chad thought she would stab everywhere except the right place and overturn the wheelchair in the process, but then, suddenly, the twitches slowed down to a trembling as, with great deliberation, she moved her head forward and jabbed at the keyboard.

'H . . . i . . . C . . . h . . . a . . . d.'

'How could she do that?' gasped Chad. 'I didn't know Sophie could read or recognise letters!'

'I've been teaching her for years,' said Mrs Walcott joyfully. 'But I didn't know whether or not she had learned anything either – not until we got this computer. For years I've been using flash cards, putting up labels around her room, writing sentences and saying them slowly in front of her. I always knew she understood. I was sure of it. Now everyone can see!'

Chad had observed, but not understood the significance of what Sophie's mother had been doing all those years. He had got used to the alphabet frieze which surrounded Sophie's bed, the letters and pictures which were stuck all over the walls – the sort of things you see in infant schools but which Chad now thought were babyish. He had seen but not understood. He always thought Mrs Walcott was pretending Sophie was normal. He thought she was deluding herself that Sophie understood anything. But now, as he saw the words punched out with such effort on to the screen: 'Hi, Chad' he felt a rush of emotion. It was as if another wormhole had opened, except this time, instead of looking down into an impenetrable darkness, it was as though he had glimpsed the miracle of creation. This thrashing, gurgling, incomprehensible creature contained within itself intelligence and understanding.

Somehow, it released something inside Chad. He was able to wait only until Sophie's mother had left the room, before the tears just streamed down his face and he found himself pouring out the whole story of Natalie's disappearance down a wormhole.

7
STRONG FORCES, WEAK FORECS

Energy is the capability of doing things

Robert Barr

Sophie listened with the strange stillness of an underwater plant. Her limbs moved like tendrils in that same uncontrollable way – floating, rising and falling as if she was moved by mysterious currents. Every now and then, Chad looked into her eyes, and he felt that he had never been more understood by anyone, than he was now.

'I don't know what to do, Sophie! I don't know how to explain to anyone that she's gone – and how she went – and it's all my fault,' wept Chad.

'Ugh! Ugh!' she grunted softly, jerking her head

towards the computer.

Eagerly, Chad leaned forward and watched the screen.

'First we have to deal with forces.' The words spluttered one by one out on to the screen as Sophie jabbed at the letters of the keyboard. 'There's gravity to deal with and the electromagnetic force. Then there are the strong forces which hold everything together and the weak forces which cause radioactivity. Tell me again, in as much detail as you can, how the crack opened up.'

Chad gulped with incredulity. How could Sophie use those words? He thought she had been a cabbage all these years. Then he remembered the many people who had been on the rota to keep her amused, adults as well as children: people like Mrs Elton, who was a professor of chemistry, Dr Rayburn, who was a musicologist and Fred Dangerfield, who was an inventor, always coming up with extraordinary schemes for powering machines in an 'ecological way' – with bicycle power, wind power and water power.

Suddenly Chad understood. Everyone who had come to entertain Sophie had taught her something and Sophie had absorbed all their knowledge like a sponge. Not just absorbed it – she had understood it. 'Oh, Sophie!' Chad cried with remorse. 'I'm so sorry!'

'Why?' The word appeared on the screen.

'For thinking you were nothing but a cabbage.'

'Don't worry about it, Chad.' The words seemed to smile back at him, though her face quivered and contorted with pleasure. 'Let's try and sort out this problem. Tell me more about Professor Tlingit.'

So Chad told his story all over again, adding other details as he remembered them, and answering Sophie's questions as they came up on the screen. 'He called himself a cosmographic geomorphologist.'

'Goodness!' exclaimed Sophie. 'So he studies the structure and layout of the land as well as the cosmos.'

'Yes!' Chad gasped with amazement at Sophie's knowledge. 'He said our house was on a cosmic swamp! And he talked about wormholes – yes, wormholes!'

Suddenly, as he relived the moment when Professor Tlingit was sucked down the wormhole, Chad remembered. 'The pole!' he shouted. 'How could I forget! It's still in my room! Professor Tlingit took out a pole, a rod – well, a sort of music stand with an antenna-type thing on the end of it, to help find the exact spot in my room where the crack had opened up. He called it a "wormhole detector". Yes, that's it!'

'Wormholes?' Sophie only just managed to repeat the word on the screen, before her body went into a paroxysm of uncontrollable jerking so that she couldn't go on.

'It did strange things. Maybe it was the rod that made him – or was it her? – float up to the ceiling. It was all so peculiar, like a dream. That's why I haven't been remembering things clearly. But I think it's still in my room. I remember now, it was in my hand when the professor was sucked away.'

'Bring it!' Sophie wrapped her arms round herself to keep her body under control. She stabbed again at the keyboard, stumbling in her excitement. 'Bring it, bring it, bring it!'

Chad stood up and looked down into Sophie's eager eyes. 'I'll go and get it, but –' He hesitated and felt a twinge of fear tug at his guts. 'You don't think it will open up that . . . that wormhole . . . and drag me down as it did the professor, do you?' But before Sophie could turn to the keyboard to respond, Chad laughed shakily. 'That's an unanswerable question, isn't it? I'll go and get it, but, if I don't come back, you'll know what's happened!'

He spoke with a wry grin, but he caught a flash of unease in Sophie's eyes. 'Be careful,' they said.

'I'll be careful,' answered Chad.

As he left the house, he heard Sophie's mother singing in the kitchen.

> *Speed, bonnie boat, like a bird on the wing,*
> *'Onward,' the sailors cry:*
> *Carry the lad that's born to be king*
> *Over the sea to Skye.*

8
LETTING GO

Has time a reality outside the human mind?

'I don't quite understand what you are,' said Natalie.
'I don't understand . . . that's a strange way of
putting things, isn't it?' she said, half to herself. 'Is
there such a thing as overstand?'

She felt a strange humming through her hands
holding on to the cord which joined them all
together. It must have been more than just a cord. It
was umbilical: it seemed to enable each of them that
held it to communicate. It seemed to feed them,
unite them, hold them together to enable them to
survive in the different states into which they went.

They had entered a cave made of ice. It arched

over their heads, dazzling white, glistening with crystals. Beyond was the deadly blue of the sea. Why did she think it was deadly? Some pre-knowledge? Something she'd heard about someone falling into water in sub-zero temperatures? Once in the water, it meant death; either dying of cold more slowly by staying in the water, or quickly by coming out into even colder temperatures on land which froze you solid in a few seconds.

How strange then, that there were creatures that could survive such temperatures. Even as she thought it, one of the wormholers let go the cord and plunged into the water.

Natalie screamed. She couldn't help it. She felt her body jerk instinctively to go and help, but another wormholer whispered, 'It's all right. He has reached his goal. It's where he belongs. That's why he let go.'

'What do you mean, his goal? What was his goal? How can he belong in a freezing sea. Is he dead? Did he belong to death?'

There was no answer for a very long time. The wormholers just continued, moving at random.

'Am I dead?' The cord throbbed in her hands.

'There is no death. Only existence or nonexistence. And where one exists, others might not be able to exist. We each have our own states and our own time. There is a time-scale to everything, but we don't always know what it is or why. One minute something is here, the next it is gone. Something exists – for a second or an hour or a day or for three hundred years – and then it ceases. We don't know how long you will stay with us. Some of us have been worming for hundreds of years, but others come and go as quickly as a meteorite flaring in the sky.'

'I want to exist,' Natalie's whole being pleaded, but she couldn't quite remember why. What was the point of existence? What had she been before the wormholers?

'You were in a state of being and it was meaningful to you.'

Her body absorbed the information like a plant absorbing moisture and sunlight. 'Yes,' she murmured.

'You may find another state of being which is meaningful, then you can release your hold on this cord and enter into it. It happens. Sometimes.'

'How will I know?' asked Natalie.

'How does a baby know when to be born?' came the reply. 'You just know, that's all. Then you let go.'

An image rushed into her mind, so fast that she didn't have time to comprehend it. She stood at the top of a ladder which descended into a cold swimming pool. She hung there, dithering. She wanted to swim, but dreaded the shock of the cold water which she would first have to endure. She dipped in a toe and shuddered. She took a step up the ladder but, being unwilling to give up, stepped back down again. She seemed to do that over and over again, caught in a time-loop of uncertainty. She heard her father's voice shouting, 'Natalie, let go! Just let go!'

'What happened?' asked a wormholer, reading her flash of memory. 'Did you let go?'

'I don't remember.' Natalie frowned with the effort.

'No,' murmured her companion. 'Wormholers can never remember anything they want to. They only experience the unjogged memory, which gleams unannounced and goes again.'

'I had a father once,' remembered Natalie.

They moved on.

Natalie didn't think about memory again for a while until one of those odd jerks on the cord and the sensation of being sucked through a tube brought them out into a place so familiar, she almost choked with the realisation.

'I have been here before,' she gasped. 'Should I let go?'

'If it feels right . . .' the wormholers murmured.

'I'm afraid.' Natalie was afraid. She didn't know why. On the one hand, here she was in a place so familiar, she could almost have said she was home again. Yet still she hung on to the cord.

'We're moving on,' said the wormholers. 'We never stay more than a few moments. We always move on. Only those who feel they belong let go and stay. If you don't let go now, you may lose your chance for aeons of time.'

Natalie's fingers, which had been closed into fists round the cord, loosened fractionally, then tightened again.

'Do I belong?' she asked.

'Only you can know that,' came the answer.

'I wish . . . I wish . . .'

'What do you wish?'

'I wish I wasn't alone.'

'Alone? Oh dear. You do have a lot to learn. What do you mean by alone? Is a molecule ever alone?

That's all you are. A little miniscule floating part of a giant whole which has become separated.'

She had a flash of memory again. There she was, still hanging on to the steps down into the swimming pool. Her father stood below with arms outstretched to catch her, his body refracting in water and light. Her hands gripped the rails, then she let go.

A child's voice called her name. 'Nata . . . lee! Come over here! There are hundreds!'

Blackberries. Natalie knew the voice was talking about blackberries.

'Where?' cried Natalie, and let go the cord.

Even as she did, she changed her mind and tried to grab the cord again, but the wormholers trailed round the broad girth of an oak tree-trunk and were suddenly gone.

Natalie rushed over to the tree. She circled it in a panic, beating at the great torso with her fists, panting and whimpering with fright. 'Don't leave me. It was a mistake, I wasn't ready to let go. Please wait for me.' But when a wormhole closes up, there is no trace left of it, and she finally came to an exhausted stop, sliding down to a crouching position, leaning against the tree-trunk, trying to find comfort in its solidity.

'Natalie!' The voice came again, young and shrill.

'Where are you?' she called hesitantly. She wasn't sure if she had recognised the voice who had called her name.

Fearfully, yet with such hope, she found herself walking along a grassy track. But it was as though she walked in a dream, for although she faced forwards, she found she was moving backwards. 'I'll understand soon,' she said out loud. 'I'm just confused about something.' Though what she was confused about, she couldn't quite think.

She continued like this along a path which ran rough and meandering into a veritable jungle of brambles, blood-thick with blackberries. 'I know this place!' she cried out loud, her voice shaking with pleasure and relief. Perhaps, after all, she had been right to let go. Everything was so familiar. Of course! This was where they came for holidays staying with old Great-uncle Julian on his farm. She felt a rush of elation.

'I'm coming!' she called out, still uncertain who had shouted her name.

She saw a particular cluster of berries – deep red, almost black, right in the very middle of a thorny bush. She stood on tiptoe, stretching her arm out. She felt the thorns clawing into her shorts, trapping her as if trying to draw her in. She struggled for balance, the thorns lacerating her legs. Her fingers closed round the blackberries and wriggled them off, oozing their juice into the palms of her hands. The juice mingled with bright red spots of blood glinting on the paler skin of her underarm, then, as she brushed along a briar bristling with spikes, the scratches appeared and disappeared.

'There's something wrong!' Natalie was calling. 'I bleed before I am scratched.'

'There's a pond through the woods where we can swim and wash ourselves clean,' called the voice.

'Yes, I remember,' cried Natalie. 'But we swam first, then picked the blackberries. That's the funny thing. I can remember forwards and backwards. I've done all this before. How? When? What's happening? I don't know where I am. Am I now, or then or . . .?' She felt a rush of confusion. 'We've made the blackberry pie. I remember weighing them and boiling them with sugar and rolling out the pastry, yet that came before the picking – just as the blood sprang up before I was scratched.'

She saw a very young child sitting on the shore of the lake, her legs dangling in the water.

'Are you going to swim?' asked the child.

'I'm not sure,' answered Natalie. 'Where's your mummy? Isn't it dangerous for you to be here alone?' Natalie looked around for others.

'Oh, I'm not yet at the stage when I need my parents to be around all the time. Give us a chance. Do I look that helpless?' laughed the child.

Natalie shrugged with puzzlement. 'Gosh! My parents will never let me near water alone even now when I'm eleven. You can't be more than six or seven!' Yet it was odd how the child talked more like an adult. She looked hard at the girl's face. 'Do I know you?'

'Perhaps,' the child answered. 'I'm sure we've met before. Years ago, when I was old. Yes . . .' She seemed to be struggling to remember. 'You're Natalie. At least, you look like Natalie. But of course you can't be. Natalie was nearly a baby. I looked after her till her expiry date when she re-entered into the birth state.'

'But I am Natalie,' insisted Natalie. 'I don't understand what you're talking about. How can you know me and why do I think I know you?' She frowned as she looked intently at the child. 'Why do I know you? Where have we met?'

'We met in the back time,' the child said, as if she were not quite sure herself. She kicked at the water and the spray sparkled. 'I could swim yesterday, but I can't today. Isn't it terrible? Just like that. One minute you can and the next you can't. It's terrible to have to become young.'

'I don't understand. What do you mean "become young"?'

The child glared at her as if wondering how Natalie could be so stupid. 'When is your existence day?'

'My birthday, you mean?' asked Natalie.

The child shuddered. 'That's a silly joke.'

'I don't understand. Truly. I don't think I should be here, but I am. We seem to know each other, yet for me it's all wrong. The wrong time and the wrong place. I'm scared.' Natalie looked at the young child and wondered why her face contained so much wisdom, as though she had been born with perfect knowledge and understanding. 'Mine is March the twenty-fifth, nineteen –'

'Don't tell me!' The child recoiled. 'It's bad

luck to tell anyone your expiry date.'

Natalie laughed. Her laughter rang around the woods. Pigeons seemed to be sucked out of the sky into the branches, their wings flapping noisily. 'You make me sound like a pot of yogurt in a supermarket.'

When she had stopped laughing, she became quiet. The child had hardly moved. She sat, staring into the water, tracing circles with her toe, causing delicate ripples; ripples which, curiously enough, flowed inwards from an outer edge.

'How old are you?' asked Natalie, confused by this adult child.

'If you mean how old was I when I gained entry – I was eighty-five years old on August the ninth, nineteen eighteen. I have seven years left to my expiry date. Yesterday I could swim, today I can't.' A huge tear glistened on her cheek. 'Isn't nature cruel to force us towards infancy? I hate the thought of having to be dependent.' Then, suddenly, she leapt to her feet. 'It's time to come. Bye!' And the child was off – facing forwards, but moving backwards.

Natalie didn't follow. Something was terribly wrong. She stayed by the water in a confused daze, trying to think it out. It was a long time before she understood.

When she did understand, she began whimpering with fright. She rushed round the tree in a blind panic, yelling to the wormholers. 'Come and get me out of here! Come and save me.' She hammered at the gnarled rough trunk till her knuckles bled. 'I don't want to go back to being a baby. I haven't grown up yet and I've been trying to grow up all my life!'

Natalie realised that she had stepped into her mirror universe where time was running in reverse. Bit by bit, like a slowly reverse-winding tape, her life was running backwards. Second by second, minute by minute and hour by hour, she was growing younger and younger. In this universe, life began with death and ended in birth.

9
THE UNCERTAINTY PRINCIPLE

The mass of a particle increases with its velocity
Albert Einstein

There was a suffocating stillness in the house when Chad returned. As he opened the front door, the dread of Natalie's disappearance flooded over him again. The excitement of communicating with Sophie and being able to discuss everything with her, had, for the moment, made him forget. Now, stepping into the hall, the rooms seemed to resonate with puzzled, fearful emptiness.

'Angie?' he called out instinctively then stopped, amazed that he had actually wanted to see her. 'Anyone home?' He forced his voice to sound casual and uncaring. He wished she would answer. For the first time, he wished she would poke her head out of the kitchen and give him her usual, determinedly welcoming grin – even though she knew that he would ignore it with a scowl and thunder up to his room. But no one answered. Angie must be out searching for Natalie so, uneasily, he climbed the stairs towards his bedroom.

His door was slightly ajar and he hesitated for a while, peering inside, but reluctant to cross the threshold. Suddenly, everything that had been completely familiar was now alien and terrifying. He hoped, for a fleeting second, that somehow it had all been a funny kind of day-dream, but the empty uncarpeted floor with just the bit of fringe sticking out proved that a crack had opened up in his room barely an hour ago and sucked away Professor Tlingit.

The professor's wormhole detector lay near by where it had fallen. Chad was too scared to step further into his room to retrieve it. He raced downstairs to the garden and pulled the rake out of the shed. It was long enough for him to stretch from the doorway to the rod and drag it in.

He lay on his stomach and managed to flip the rake on the far side of the detector. Then he pulled, expecting to draw the thing easily to him. But, to his amazement, it hardly budged. He pulled and heaved and finally got to his feet and used his full weight to try and get it to budge. But he might just as well have been trying to shift a fallen oak.

He gave up and got to his feet. He stared at the rod. More puzzlement. Everything was a puzzle. He kicked the doorway with irritation. He looked at his computer. He could see Professor Tlingit's calling-card disk gleaming on the side. No good using that now, was there? he thought bitterly. Yet, perhaps . . . there had been so many totally inexplicable happenings, that he shouldn't rely on normal logic. Perhaps Professor Tlingit could be contacted with the card no matter where he/she was – even down a wormhole.

Chad put out a foot over the threshold and tested his weight on the floor. He still felt an overwhelming sense of panic that any moment he could be sucked away. He stamped his foot hard. The floor felt solid enough, so he stepped inside, but kept his back to the wall. He was certainly not going to risk walking across the room to his computer. Instead, he began to shuffle tentatively, one step at a time, following the skirting board round the edge of the room, keeping his back firmly against the reassuring hard wall.

He got to within arm's length of his computer. The disk beckoned. He knew this was the logical thing to do, to try it. Taking a deep breath, he jumped away from the side of the wall and grabbed his table.

'Good heaven's, Chad! What the dickens are you doing?' His father stood in the doorway, laughing yet puzzled at his son's antics. He crossed the threshold –

'Dad! Don't!' Chad yelled a warning.

'What's the matter, son?' Chad's father continued across the room, calmly walking right over the spot where both Natalie and Professor Tlingit had plunged from sight.

Chad froze, his mouth still open. But nothing happened.

'Where is everyone?' demanded his father. 'I can't find Angie or Natalie and where've you been? The house looks like the *Marie Celeste*.'

Yes, the *Marie Celeste*, thought Chad. It was like that. Perhaps the people on that boat also got sucked away down a black hole, leaving no trace of themselves. Just the boat left floating on the ocean with its half-eaten meals and the chairs pushed back as if everyone had just popped out for a moment.

'Chad?' His father's voice broke impatiently into his thoughts. 'What's wrong with you, boy? I'm talking to you. Where is everyone?'

'Er . . . I think . . . well, Natalie should be with Sophie, but she isn't, so I am – but I've just come back to get something and Mum's probably gone to find Natalie and I expect they'll be back in a moment . . . I think . . . and I'm just off back to Sophie's. Bye, Dad.'

He finished lamely, as his father turned with exasperation and left the room again muttering. 'I don't know what this household's coming to. Everyone's going mad.'

The fact that his father had managed to walk in and out of the room without being sucked away, gave Chad more confidence. He switched on his computer and pulled up a chair. He took the calling card disk and slotted it in. The screen swirled into a snowstorm. It spluttered and beeped and emitted the strangest of sounds. It looked as though a picture was trying to break through. It could have been a heaving ocean, with spray flying across the screen. A face appeared. It seemed to bob out of the ocean up against the screen, then broke up into millions of fuzzy dots. He heard a voice but so muffled and distorted that he wasn't sure. 'I don't know what to do,' groaned Chad out loud.

'Pick up my wormhole detector, Chad. Pick up the rod.' This time he was able to distinguish the words through the fuzz.

'Is it you, professor? Is it you? Where are you? Is Natalie with you?' Chad yelled joyfully.

'Yes, it's me. I got separated from my detector and I must have it back. So pick it up, boy!'

'Professor, professor! Where are you? Are you near? Somewhere here? What about Natalie? Have you found her?'

'Stop asking questions. I can't do anything without the rod, so pick it up and be quick about it! Go on, Chad. Move,' the professor urged impatiently as Chad continued to sit riveted with relief and excitement.

'I can't, damn it! I've tried,' Chad cried desperately. 'It won't budge.'

'It will if you just pick it up with your fingers, silly boy!'

Even through the splutter and hiss of the screen, Chad could hear Professor Tlingit's cutting sarcasm. It roused his anger. 'Stupid git! Look!' Chad strode across the room and grasped the rod. To his amazement, it was as easy as picking up a walking stick.

'Silly boy!' he heard the professor sigh through the crackle.

A throb, like an electric current, ran from Chad's fingertips all the way down into the soles of his feet. Something made him leap to the side again, the rod clutched in his hand. He almost fainted with awe, as a hole flicked open in the middle of his room, like a burning eye, then closed again. He turned himself facewards to the wall and sank to his knees, pressing his forehead against its hard cold surface.

'Go with it, Chad! Go with it! Extend the rod. Bring it to me,' Professor Tlingit's voice urged from the computer.

He/she must be mad. Go down the black hole – just like that? Chad felt he was swimming in fear and mistrust. The professor only seemed to care about getting the rod back. Nothing about Natalie or how they would find her. Chad felt paralysed with confusion, unable to breathe, move or think. Only his heart thudded with a will of its own.

'Wait . . . wait . . .' Chad whispered, half to the professor and half to his inner self. 'Give me a chance. Just give me a chance while I think what to do.' He fought with his panic and his jumbling thoughts. He chewed his lip obsessively and concentrated on the feel of the rod in his hand. He couldn't tell whether the throb he felt in his fist was the rod's power or his own blood pulsating. Boom, boom, boom! He tuned into its rhythm and let it steady his breathing. Then he got to his feet and walked purposefully back to the desk. Professor Tlingit's face was clearer now. It grinned at him, trying to look friendly and reassuring. Yet Chad was not reassured.

'Trust me, Chad. Extend the rod and bring it to me. No harm will come to you and we can then look for Natalie.'

Chad hid his eyes. Suddenly he couldn't bear the sight or sound of the professor any more. He needed time to think. 'I'll contact you again from Sophie's!' Chad cried with lowered eyes. 'I'm going now.'

'No, Chad! Don't switch me off! Don't even think of it, you blithering idiot! No, no, n–!' Silence. The screen went to blank as, with a thrust of his hand, Chad switched off the computer.

Chad was shaking all over. How could he have done it? He chewed his lip fiercely, stunned by his own defiance, and stared at the rod. How ordinary it looked. Could it really contain so much power?

At last, he forced himself into action. He pocketed the computer disk and, feeling more in control than he had ever done since Natalie's disappearance, returned to Sophie's house.

He had never seen Sophie so still. Her eyes were fixed at the screen in front of her. It was filled with figures and calculations. He paused watching her for a moment. Her claw-like hands were raised as if in surprise; her head was thrown back, her mouth twisted and open. Then she heard him, and the spell was broken. Her body quivered uncontrollably. She moved her head towards the keyboard. She selected a clear screen and wrote, 'I was afraid.'

Chad came and stood where their eyes could meet. He saw Sophie's brimming with relief. He triumphantly held out the wormhole detector. 'I got

it back. I made contact with the professor again –
with this.' He held out the disk. Sophie writhed and
jerked with excitement. 'But I switched him off.
Did I do wrong? He was going on at me. Got me
mad. I . . .'

'Don't worry,' Sophie wrote. 'Just tell me what
happened.'

'The professor wanted me to give him the rod,
but I wasn't going to go down that black hole. He
must be mad. I couldn't just go. I don't know . . . I
don't know if I trust him, or is it her? I don't even
know if the professor's male or female. All he wanted
was the rod. How do I know that she won't just dump
me the minute she gets it? She's so weird. I just don't
know if he/she's good or bad, friend or enemy. She
doesn't care about Natalie –' Chad stopped short as
he heard himself.

'I'm glad *you* care about Natalie, Chad,' tapped
Sophie.

Chad gave an embarrassed laugh. 'Well, I care
that she's disappeared into nowhere. I mean, I have
to care, don't I? She is family – sort of – and it's my
fault she's gone. Anyway, I've got to get her back,
otherwise there'll be all hell to pay. I mean, Angie

will go mad. This rod is all I've got. If this rod has the power to find her, then I'll keep hold of it, and if the professor wants her rod back, she'll just have to help me.'

Chad held the rod out before Sophie for her to see.

Her eyes gleamed bright with fierce curiosity. 'W . . . w . . . w . . .!' She wanted to say the word. 'Wormholes!'

Chad slid the rod across Sophie's arm so that she felt its touch against her skin. She quivered with excitement and longed to grasp it – this 'wormhole detector'. She wanted to hold it, revolve it in her hands, examine it minutely, if only her writhing limbs would let her. She turned to her screen and jabbed out the questions which burned in her brain. 'How long is it? How thick is it? How heavy is it?'

She had to rely on Chad to describe its texture and all its features. She became particularly excited when he described how he had tried to rake it in; how it seemed rooted to the floor and too heavy to move, yet when he had picked it up with his hands, it was as light as a walking stick.

'What is it made of?' Sophie asked on the screen.

'I'm not sure,' murmured Chad. 'I no sooner think it's aluminium, then it seems more like plastic. Then when I think it may be some kind of wood, I decide it's probably lead because it is heavy. But I no sooner think it's heavy, than it becomes as light as a feather and I change my mind and think it's an alloy of some sort.'

He held it up to the window. 'Look, it could be hollow when you hold it up to the light.' Then he lowered it and looked again.

'Weigh it,' ordered Sophie. 'I need to know as much about it as possible. I've been trying to work on some calculations in quantum mechanics to do with particles and antiparticles. The sum over sum of the probabilities of the positions and speed of discrete particles. It's the uncertainty principle: you can't know the speed of a particle and its exact position at the same time. It's like taking a photograph of a racing car. You make a choice. Either you photograph its speed, in which case you have a blurred picture of light and shape, or else you photograph the car itself, in which case you have all the details of the car but no realisation of its speed. It's just a fact of nature. You can't know both things at once.' Sophie learned back with her eyes closed. Trying to communicate with Chad had exhausted her.

Chad paced the room. He felt stupid and ignorant. How could she know all this? It was too much. He kept coming back and leaning over her shoulder to try and understand her thoughts which sprawled across the screen in words and calculations.

'I think . . .' At last, Sophie leaned forward again and began to tap. 'I think the rod is made of variable particles which perhaps divide and subtract themselves but come back together again. Sometimes a particle will do something unexpected. That's why the weight varies. To preserve weight, movement and energy have to be conserved. Einstein worked out that the mass of a particle increases with its velocity. I wonder if it's possible to conserve momentum across multiple universes?'

Chad sighed with incomprehension and went to the bathroom. He found the bathroom scales and lugged them back. Sophie had tapped out more.

'We know what particles are in the gross state, like our planet revolving round the sun, but not in the particular – so we don't know what any individual particle or person on our planet will do. It's hard to determine what is most probable to happen . . .'

'Shut up, shut up, shut up!' Chad suddenly yelled in anger. 'I don't know what you're talking about!' Then he covered his head with remorse. 'Oh, Sophie, I'm sorry. It's all beyond me. Just gobbledegook!' wailed Chad in despair. 'What am I going to do about Natalie?'

'Perhaps the rod contains gravitons,' Sophie ignored his outburst, and rapidly tapped out her thoughts, 'a kind of gravity-exchange force which can defy one kind of gravity and be attracted to another. Perhaps that's how it detects wormholes. We just don't know. We can't know everything we want to know about particles because each particle seems to have a mind of its own. If I can only work out the position of the hole in your room and the velocity with which the professor descended . . . then I could work out a probability . . .' Her tapping stopped mid-sentence as if her voice had trailed away.

'This is all too much,' gasped Chad, shaking his head in confusion. 'What are you talking about?'

Sophie didn't answer but urged him to put the rod on to the bathroom scales. 'Weigh it three times,' she said.

'It's unbelievable,' he muttered, as each time it weighed something completely different.

Sophie's body swung and shuddered with intense excitement. A trickle of saliva coiled out of the side of her mouth. She jabbed fiercely at the keyboard. 'I must feel it again. Touch it. Help me.'

Chad pulled Sophie's chair around then, standing behind her, he held the rod at each end and lifted it over her head and in front of her. He took first one of her jerking hands and, closing his hand over the top of hers, gripped the rod. He did the same to the other.

Her body leapt almost out of her chair. It was as if she was riven with electricity. Welded together, their hands jerked up and down with the rod and her body twisted and writhed as if in agony. Desperately, Chad tried to wrench it from her grasp, but she wouldn't or couldn't let go. Her fingers were clenched round it like rigor mortis.

In their struggle, her wheelchair careered round the room, dragging Chad with it. It knocked over tables and chairs, and lunged back and forth and round in circles. Finally, with a sudden acceleration, it headed for the far wall. Chad yelled desperately, as he tried to yank the chair away from its perilous course, but it hurtled forwards. He flung himself over Sophie to protect her from the inevitable impact. But, instead of the crash he had expected, he felt his stomach turn over, as the chair swooped up the side of the wall like a roller-coaster and finally stopped upside down on the ceiling – just as he'd done with the professor.

'Sophie!' he managed to shriek, as a black hole opened beneath them. They plunged down.

There was a sucking, squelching, squeezing sensation and a feeling that he must fill his lungs with air or die. But though his mouth opened, Chad could make no sound. Clamped together, Chad, Sophie in her wheelchair and the rod still clasped in their hands, were first slithering and tumbling, rolling and bouncing; then were being forced down a passage so narrow, that their limbs were wrapped round their bodies.

He was aware of the surfaces: surfaces which were as wet and wobbly as jelly, surfaces which had no grip, nothing uneven to impede their progress.

Briefly he slowed down as the passage narrowed even more, but now there was a sensation of being crushed, stretched and drawn. They were being pulled by a great force, tugged through a space so small, he thought they must have all their bones crushed to a pulp. This is what it must be like to be swallowed by a python or a boa constrictor, he thought. This is what it must be like to be born.

Within a second, it was all over. A burst of cold air struck them as they were expelled into space. Air rushed into their open mouths. Their bodies were ejected and they slipped out like fish, flapping and gasping in an exhausted heap.

'Ah, ah, ah, ah, ahhhhhh!' The sound of his own voice shrieking filled his ears.

Chad felt naked, helpless, unbearably alone. 'Mum! Mum! I want my mum!' he bayed like a wild animal. His arms flailing around – unswaddled, unembraced, unheld, unloved. The sense of abandonment engulfed him like a wave. 'I want my mother,' he bellowed and raged. He was sure he could feel her presence, smell her, hear her voice as she rocked him, newly born, in her arms. His mouth rooted around to suck and feed; his whole being raged against being cast out from that small ocean within that small universe which had been his mother. He rolled around, curling himself up into a tight ball. Trying to pretend he had never been born. Trying to recapture the feeling of being safe and anchored until sheer exhaustion finally plunged him into a deep sleep.

10
GOPHER

The more a body falls less slowly, the less its speed is greater

A book arched downwards, its pages fluttering as it fell. Objects of every kind from odd socks to Biros, car keys to old refrigerators rained in, or were ejected upwards from cracks in the ground.

A single trainer hurtled through the air. That's when he saw the creature. It appeared from nowhere and with an outstretched tentacle caught the trainer. The creature was not quite human, not quite animal. Its skin was smooth yet rumpled into podgy folds, protruding into fat limbs and merging into a smooth round featureless head, like a worm. It was darting

90

about trying to catch as many objects as it could before they struck the ground and stuffing them into a sack which it dragged around. As the creature worked, it whistled, casual as a workman on a building site.

Chad clasped his arms round his knees and rocked to and fro. The roly-poly creature moved with the clumsy energy of a newborn grub. It seemed able to extend and retract its limbs at will, snatching at objects, stuffing them into its bottomless pit of a sack.

Suddenly the whistling stopped and the creature halted in its tracks. Something had seized its attention. It had seen Sophie, strapped into her chair.

Panic brought Chad stumbling to his feet. 'Sophie!' He thought he yelled her name, but couldn't hear his own voice.

Her head was flung back and her mouth open. She was utterly still. He had never seen her still, never seen her when there wasn't one limb waving around, or her head constantly rolling this way and that. 'Sophie! Don't be dead, please don't be dead!' He tried again to cry out but, as in a nightmare, it was like shouting underwater.

A long piercing whistle came from the creature. With a giant spring, it landed right at Sophie's side.

'Mine, mine! This is mine and this is mine and this is mine too!' Chad didn't know how he understood, but he knew what the creature was saying.

A pair of spectacles was ejected out of a squelchy tube. They tumbled through the air, some kind of light refracting and sparkling through the lenses. 'Mine, mine!' chortled the creature. Its podgy arm extended, as swift as a snake's tongue, and swiped the spectacles down into its sack. Then it turned its attention back to Sophie. It whooshed round in circles, gurgling with excitement and grabbed the wheelchair.

Obviously items like this didn't come its way too often. It clambered all over Sophie and the chair, examining every detail. 'What is this? What is this? And what is this?' It fingered the wheels, the spokes, the arms and the buttons and the computer screen which was still on and flickering.

Then it turned its attention to Sophie herself. 'What is this? What is this? And what is this?' It flicked at her hair, poked its fingers up her nose and in her ears. It opened and shut her eyelids and moved her head around. Sophie didn't stir.

Suddenly it was behind her. First it rocked her violently, as if discovering how to move her, then, with a kind of shrug, it enveloped her with one arm, pulled open the mouth of the sack with the other and thrust her inside.

The creature was running now at a great speed, dragging the sack behind it: faster, faster, faster.

'Sophie! Come back, come back! Wait for me!' Chad lurched forward in a desperate attempt to follow, but his body didn't know what to do, and he just flailed around helplessly.

It was a landscape of crinkles and ridges, strange mounds and growths. There were pools of still, shining water, reflecting shapes that could be birds and trees. The sky, if sky it was, looked the same as the land, as if one mirrored the other and it was impossible to tell which was real and which a reflection. There was no up or down, but spirals and curves which criss-crossed and turned into sharp angles and chequered squares. There were humps and hillocks and deep ditches yet, strangely, the land was as flat as a game board, without any obvious direction. Chad couldn't tell how he should move across such a surface or where he should aim for.

'I want to go home,' he howled, and rolled himself up into a tight ball.

A dark blob gathered on a silver-lined horizon, at first small but then increasing in size. As it grew, it contorted, expanded and contracted like an infinitely malleable substance. Parts of it broke away and created its own formations.

Chad opened one eye and watched but didn't move. The blob was made up of millions of tiny individual parts. He remembered flocks of birds at evening, moving in swarms as if in some kind of dance or game, separating, swooping apart, arching upwards, downwards then hurtling back towards each other and making up a whole once more.

Behind them was the silver light of the horizon, before them was a gold light – from where it came he couldn't tell. He marvelled at the length and breadth of the space before him and the strange formation. It came nearer and nearer, changing from silver to gold and gold back to silver as it tipped and looped and swirled.

Then his head was filled with singing as the blob descended on him like a shower of glistening raindrops. It swept over his skin, rumpled through his hair. It soothed, beguiled.

Chad listened. He felt himself lifted up and carried. 'Where are we going?' he cried.

'Wormholing!' came the answer.

They closed round him so densely that he merged into them, all his molecules moving as part of a greater solid body, his mind becoming part of a greater mind.

For a while they swarmed like this across a wide surface, swooping and swirling, till, suddenly, the blob he had become a part of broke up. Chad's body and mind disintegrated and his particles scattered in different directions. The whole of eternity opened up to him like a yawning mouth.

'Look what I can see!' cried Chad.

Bits of him flew up into the galaxies, mingled with exploding stars, and bubbled with newly formed planets. He saw earthquakes thrusting up mountain ranges, the tectonic plates of continents colliding, and volcanos spewing fire and liquid metal out of the bowels of the earth. He saw rivers and oceans and jungles and deserts. He saw cities of glass and villages of mud – and suddenly he saw his own town.

'I know that!' he shouted. It was his own neighbourhood. 'I live there! Look! I know that. That's my road, the shop, my school.'

The scene came closer to him and he got even more excited. There was a house and a garden. 'Is that me?' he asked. 'Hey, that is me! Look at me! Look! I'm trying to dribble the football. That was my first football and there's my dad. Dad!' he yelled till he thought his lungs would burst. 'Don't move on. Can't I stay a while?' But he tumbled on. 'Who's that?'

A fully grown man strode down a road – still trying to avoid the cracks on the pavement.

'It's you,' the wormholers told him.

'How can it be me when I'm here and I'm not grown up?' Chad was mystified.

'Consider the possibility that there is no single time for something to happen; that time can bend and stretch backwards and forwards and round; and that time past and time future can overlap and even run parallel to time present. Consider that there may be many times happening together.

'That's the joy of wormholing. You can exist on all time planes at once. You can go back or forwards whenever you like. It's up to you.'

He whirled through time as if it were a merry-go-round. He was a baby, a boy, a man and a grandfather. But something was missing. 'Something's missing,' he said.

'If there is, only you know about it. You'll only see what your mind wants to,' said the wormholers.

'What does it all mean?' Chad asked, feeling dazed. 'Where do I belong now?'

'We heard you crying that you wanted to go home, so home is where you want to be.'

He was descending. Chad thought 'home'. He felt an old anger surge through him. Below him, he saw what home had once been. 'That used to be home,' he murmured bitterly. Then he remembered. 'It's Mum who's missing.'

Once, he thought he was sure of home, when they were one happy family – Mum and Dad and him. Then Mum left. 'Don't go, don't go,' he heard himself crying out. But she went anyway.

'Look after things while I'm away,' she told Chad.

And there he was, looking after things. Chad saw himself from a different plane. He was patrolling what had been their territory, like a faithful watch-dog, protecting their space till she should return. Each room had its function and its meaning, each wall and pavement stone marked out their neighbourhood.

But she didn't return. No amount of explanations could help. And now there was Dad, Angie and Natalie.

Home faded like an old photograph and the hole inside him, which had once been filled with certainty, emptied and filled again with grief and fury.

'I love my dad,' he told the wormholers. 'But I love my mother too.'

The scene faded abruptly.

Below them spread a vast ocean. He saw the white spray of fountains spurting out of the waves. His eyes cleared of tears and he forgot the past.

'Whales!' he yelled excitedly. 'Oh, look at the whales!' There was a whole school of them, lazily lounging just below the translucent blue surface, picking up the shadows of clouds which fleeted across their great, grey backs.

'Do you belong with whales?' asked the wormholers.

'It's where I want to be,' answered Chad as all his particles came together again.

11
A PLACE WHERE YOU BELONG

Symmetry is all important in nature

Donald Francis Tovey

Sophie was tumbling in ever expanding spaces. The inside of the sack was like another universe, on and on ... She found herself orbiting in a ring containing all sorts of junk. There were other rings too, like the rings of Saturn. Some were made up of meteors, exploded stars and old spaceships. Other revolving rings contained more familiar items: odd shoes, socks, single gloves, bits of Lego, pencils and Biros, calculators and keys – all the sorts of things which get so easily lost or mislaid. All those things about which one might say: 'I could have sworn I had a . . .' or 'I know I put it here . . .' or 'I think there must be a black hole somewhere out there which sucks away . . .'

'Look what I found!' a voice chortled and, suddenly, she was tipped out.

She felt as if she were strapped to the sails of a windmill. She turned up and round and down and, though her eyes were closed, colours merged and mingled behind her lids.

'It has your rod!' chattered the voice. 'That's why I came to you.'

'My rod, Gopher! You've found my wormhole detector!' a voice burbled like liquid. 'Thank goodness I have it back. I can't believe it. Did Chad bring it back? Where is he? Who is this? Has Chad come wormholing from the other universe?'

Sophie felt herself turned round.

'But this isn't Chad.' The voice sounded mystified.

'Chad!' Sophie's eyes flew open at the sound of his name. She tried to speak but only squawked. She leaned forward desperately and jabbed her headstick on to the computer keyboard. 'Where's Chad?'

A strange face bobbed before her – smoothly grey, with two small, hard, round eyes, set back in a broad, curving, dolphin-like head. 'Oh dear, oh dear!' it said. The professor tried to extricate the rod from Sophie's fingers, but she held on to it with a grip of steel. Somewhere in her brain was the memory that the rod had brought them here, and maybe only the rod could get them back.

Sophie's computer screen flickered and fuzzed as the professor surveyed the situation. 'Are you Professor Tlingit?' Sophie tapped with her headstick.

'You're not Chad,' it answered.

There was a sound of rippling. Everything around her glimmered blue-green. Water. Sophie jabbed, 'I don't understand where I am.'

'Why, oh why, oh why? Why are you so stupid? You are here.' The professor's face frowned at her. 'Oh dear,' muttered the professor. 'Oh dear, oh dear, oh dear. Now we have a problem of great magnitude. Who are you and what, may I ask, is your type of life form? Are you a random particle or part of a whole entity? You are not entirely human, I take it. I am not familiar with your species.'

'I am human, and of course I'm not stupid,' Sophie added with a surge of anger. 'And I don't think I'm a random particle – though sometimes I wonder. I'm Sophie, Chad's friend.'

'Ah! Sophie. Human, but with interesting additions.' The professor did another double flip downwards then upwards. 'Sophie!' There was a heavy sigh.

'Are you Professor Tlingit?' tapped Sophie, struggling to concentrate as she continued her slow tumbling.

The professor's voice sounded like bubbles. 'It is me, it is I, though you don't deserve it to be me. It was really most rash of Chad to switch me off like that.'

She looked at the professor's strange, grey face with its hard black and impenetrable eyes. Sophie opened her mouth again. 'Ch . . . Ch . . . Ch . . .' Her voice broke out in grunts and squeals as she struggled to form words. She shook her head. The professor sounded extremely displeased and Sophie had an impression of it diving down, looping round head over heels and then wooshing up again.

'How long . . .?' Sophie's words broke across the screen more quickly. Time was the first question. 'When did we . . .? How long have I . . .?' Then, more steadily she asked, 'Did we come down a wormhole?

102

Where are we? Where is Chad? Are we dead?'

'It's no good asking questions about time or place!' Professor Tlingit's voice suddenly chuckled in her ear. 'Time and place are what you make them. Of course you're not dead. That word has no meaning anyway. There is only existence in different forms. There are only wormholes.'

The blue around her swirled as the professor circled thoughtfully. 'What a pity Chad did not exit your universe from his room as I asked him to,' grumbled Professor Tlingit. 'But at least we have the detector.'

Sophie looked down at her hands. 'The detector? Oh, the wormhole detector! Ah! This thing?' As naturally as anything, Sophie lifted it up. She felt tingles like an electric current surging through her arms. 'Look what I did!' she yelled, marvelling at her new-found power. 'Hey, look at me! Look what I can do!' Exhilarated, she waved the rod in the air. She no longer felt a prisoner of her wheelchair, any more than an arm is a prisoner of the body. 'Mum! Dad! You could lift me now!' Her body felt so light, she thought she would ascend like a balloon.

'Well, well, well! That seems to be just what you

need,' observed the professor. 'I think I know exactly the right place for you.'

'Is there a place where I could have power over myself?' asked Sophie excitedly.

In this last year, Sophie had got too heavy for her mother. Her dad had always helped her in the mornings before going to work. He had lifted her to the bathroom, washed her, dressed her and settled her in the wheelchair. But then he was gone for the rest of the day, and it was her mother who had to cope with seeing her to and from school.

One day, her mother, who had been lifting her, gasped in pain and clutched her back.

'What is it, Mum?' Sophie's inner voice had cried in sudden fear and her body twitched with alarm.

For some moments, her mother didn't speak, but rubbed her back vigorously and then tentatively straightened up. That time, the pain had cleared and her face broke into smiles again. 'Oh dear! My little Sophie! You're not so little now. You're growing and growing and getting heavy. I think I'll have to get in an elephant to lift you in and out of your chair.'

They had both laughed together at the thought, Sophie wriggling and squealing and tossing her head from side to side. But behind the laughter lay the anxiety. 'What will happen when I get too heavy for you?' she wanted to ask, but her muscles refused her even the power to communicate.

Her mother had hugged her reassuringly. 'Don't worry. We'll sort everything out step by step,' she said, as if reading her thoughts.

Instead of getting an elephant, her father rearranged his day and made sure he was home in time to help her to bed. But they had all discussed the possibility of Sophie going to a special boarding school where they had the staff and facilities to help her. Her mother and father looked excited when they talked about it. But deep down inside her secret soul, Sophie had wept. Why should I have to go away? Why can't I be at home like everyone else?

'The important thing, Sophie,' her father whispered to her one day, 'is to give you the power. Power now and power in the future.' He hadn't said any more, but she thought about it for a long time after.

Power. She had never quite understood what power was. She, whose every muscle refused her any control over it, who had to be strapped in her chair to stop her own limbs from hurling her about and who, when she heard her mother singing, longed to sing too and had shrieked in frustration – Sophie longed for power.

Here . . . she looked at her hand and her mind commanded. Lift hand. Her hand lifted. Turn head! Her head turned. She chose a direction to look; her head obeyed her desire. She chose to be still, and she was completely still.

Sophie arched her neck back and opened her mouth. 'Aaah!' A rich, clear sound burst from her throat. She held the note until her breath ran out. A line of bubbles rose upwards, sparkling. She breathed in again and exploded into song.

Speed, bonnie boat, like a bird on the wing,
'Onwards,' the sailors cry.

It had been her mother's favourite and she used to sing it while washing and dressing her. It had always made Sophie toss her head and open her mouth and try desperately to do the same. But all she had been capable of, was to emit ugly squeals and shrieks like some tortured bird.

Here, her muscles tightened and relaxed with

the song and anyone could recognise the sound which emerged.

> *Speed, bonnie boat, like a bird on the wing,*
> *'Onwards,' the sailors cry.*
> *Carry the lad that's born to be king*
> *Over the sea to Skye.*

The notes of the song tumbled around them as Sophie waved Professor Tlingit's rod.

The professor frowned. 'Don't do that. It's not a toy.'

'It lets me sing!' laughed Sophie, quivering with joy.

'This rod is my own unique invention. It's a cosmic compass – a sort of divining rod,' the professor said. 'That's how I met Chad. With it, I have been opening up wormholes into other universes and trying to plot them on a cosmic map.'

Sophie excitedly tried to speak as she had been able to sing, but it would take practice, so instead she jabbed at the keyboard again. 'Chad told me all about you. Natalie is lost and we were desperate to find her. We knew this rod was special. Did you

107

design it round the uncertainty principle?'

The professor loomed close and stared into her eyes. 'I like the human brain, when it's not being stupid.' Then Professor Tlingit unstrapped her from her chair. 'Let me explain,' the words burbled as Sophie drifted out of her chair.

Sophie was floating. She held the rod while her arms and legs flowed outwards like a ballet dancer. She twisted her wrists and exercised her fingers. She bent and stretched her legs and pirouetted round and round, twisting her neck this way and that. 'Oh, Mum! Dad! You should see me now!' she sang.

'You know that for every positive, there must be a negative,' the professor continued earnestly. 'Where there is action there must be reaction; where there is forwards, there must be backwards; where things are visible there are others which are invisible; where there is order there must be chaos. It means a constant tension between opposing forces. I invented this rod to control such forces. See how it enables you to dance? It also finds the linking wormholes that enable me to travel between all these different universes. Only with the rod can you find your way back to where you belong. It's lucky for you and me that you were collected by Gopher.'

'What do you mean, collected?' Sophie swam round to her chair and jabbed at the keyboard with her headstick. 'Collected as in picked up or collected as in stamp collection?'

'Both, actually, my dear. You were picked up by a gopher and thrown into a cosmic sack to be part of a collection for trading and exchange. Gophers can be a bit of a menace – always going for this or going for that, making a filthy mess of the cosmos, leaving their litter around, trespassing into other universal zones, collecting whatever they can lay their hands on. Gophers usually follow wormholers and go scavenging through the wormholes which are opened up. He could have taken you anywhere. But at least he recognised the rod and had the sense to bring you to me. Hmm . . .' The professor coiled and uncoiled itself into a slow, thoughtful loop. 'So, as you were collected by a gopher, Chad is probably with the wormholers.'

'Will the rod help me to find Chad and Natalie. And how do we go back?'

'Ah! A cosmic question. How,' the professor sighed, suddenly returning. Two smooth, grey hands covered her hands which held the rod. She felt herself swiftly returned to her wheelchair. 'Are you sure you want to go back?' and, sliding the rod from her hand, the professor suddenly swooped away like a whale gathering itself for a leap.

'Don't go!' Sophie opened and shut her mouth soundlessly. She jabbed frantically at the keyboard. 'Please come back. Don't leave me. I don't know what I want. Can't I just have the rod and go home?'

The screen was filled with a glistening ocean. She could see a grey body streaking just beneath the surface like the shadow of a cloud swiftly passing. With a great fountain of spray it hurtled upwards into the air and hung there for a moment before plunging back down.

Then the professor's face reappeared in big close-up on the screen. 'You are not well designed for where you are. My world is a superior place, a place far better suited for you and your brain. You are too good for that earth-sky. Your talents are wasted there. In any case, I need you. I've been looking for a genius like you to pass on my knowledge and power, for even I don't want to live forever.' Then the screen went blank.

Sophie jerked uncontrollably. She tried to hold up her hands, but they wouldn't obey and waved around. 'Come back, come back! I need the power!' The words struggled in her brain, but they wouldn't come out coherently. She bent over her keyboard, shaking and barely able to aim, but after several misses, she at last managed to prod, 'I need the power to go home.'

The words glimmered on the screen.

Sophie and her chair moved very slowly, tumbling over and over in a great, clanking, ever-expanding space. Motion was barely perceptible and went on and on and on. She opened her mouth. At first a shriek rose from her throat. Then suddenly she felt the notes of the song bubbling up.

> *Speed, bonnie boat, like a bird on the wing,*
> *'Onwards,' the sailors cry.*
> *Carry the lad that's born to be king*
> *Over the sea to Skye.*

Singing can travel like no other sound. Singing communicates like no other language. The whales deep in the ocean sing. Apes, swinging within the forest canopy, sing, passing on their tune from one to the other. Frogs and birds and insects sing; even the trunks of trees sing with the rising of the sap. The resonances of sung notes can traverse universes, colliding with stars and ricocheting off suns. They say that the spheres sing.

Singing means the drawing and expelling of breath; it means life. The egg-shaped life force which lay on the shore and could have been a pebble, stirred inside. A time-space woman gazing out to sea cried, 'I gave life once. I have a son.' And far out in the ocean she heard singing and wondered if it was a whale.

'Come on, come on, come on!' The professor returned to Sophie in a great whoosh of spray and bubbles, chortling with excitement. 'You don't want to go back to that silly old world. Come on, come on. Let's go wormholing into a glorious future. I know just the place for you.'

'I don't think so,' murmured Sophie doubtfully. 'I don't think there's any other place I want to be except home. I want to find Chad and Natalie and take them home. I don't want any other future.'

'You can't say what you don't want till you've seen what you can have,' insisted the professor, and holding her chair with one hand, he/she waved the rod with the other. 'Here we go! Wheee . . .'

12
IN THE EYE OF
THE WHALE

How inappropriate to call this planet 'Earth' when it is clearly Ocean

Arthur C. Clarke

Lyn came in from her walk by the sea. The colours had been particularly iridescent: the blue of the Pacific as luminous as sapphires and the sky paling to almost white in the full glare of the sun. She had breathed in its beauty, marvelling at it, as she did almost every day. Yet she was always left with a deep melancholy which she couldn't shake off.

She stepped into the dark cool interior of the house and glanced in the mirror. She glimpsed a face peering out behind her from a gap in the wall, between a picture and an umbrella stand.

'Chad?' She whirled round, her son's name breaking from her lips. But there was no gap, no face, nothing different from usual. She paused, feeling dazed, her heart thumping furiously. She touched the place on the wall where – where? Where what? What had she seen? The wall was hard. It must have been a trick of the light, a reflection from the glass. These days, she kept thinking that she saw her son Chad. He was a boy on the beach, braced before the waves with arms taut at his side. He was in a crowd going up an escalator. She remembered with misery how she had raced after him, seeing his head bobbing ahead of her, but he vanished before she could reach him. Chad was everywhere, awake and asleep.

She turned back to face herself in the mirror. 'Why?' she asked silently. The 'why' she asked herself was the why of a thousand thousand questions starting with 'Why am I as I am?'

She swayed slightly, feeling dizzy with her thoughts. The ground burned through her feet as if she could feel the tilt of the earth's axis keeping her at a constant distance away from her son. While it was day for her in New Zealand, it was night for Chad in

England. She wondered if, while he slept, he ever dreamed of her. She had asked him to come and live with her in New Zealand, but he had preferred to stay with his dad at home. He had never replied to her letter when she wrote to tell him that she and her new husband Pete had had a baby. Didn't it mean anything to Chad to know he had a half-brother called Ricky?

Lyn moved quietly through the house to the baby's room. She had left Ricky having his afternoon sleep in the care of his grandmother, Pete's mother. Grandma had fallen asleep in the armchair, her fingers resting on the open pages of the book she was reading.

Ricky, instead of being asleep, had pulled himself upright to a standing position, clutching the rails of his cot. His blue eyes were alert and dancing with excitement. He watched the rocking horse which his father had made for him. It was a big wooden horse, too big for him yet, but he always loved to see it rock.

Chad had suddenly appeared from a gap between the bookshelf and the toy cupboard. He leapt on to the rocking horse, making it rock violently. Ricky roared with laughter. 'More, more!' was what his babbling cry demanded.

'Why did you bring me here?' Chad asked the wormholers angrily.

'We didn't. You must have wanted to come,' they told him. 'You said you loved your mother – and that's what brought you here to her.'

'But this! I don't love this!' he snarled, pointing at the baby.

The baby just gurgled at the funny boy.

'I hate you, I hate you! Don't you understand?' Chad yelled at the baby. He stood up on the rocking horse, his arms outstretched for balance. He felt ugly and mean and wanted revenge for his pain. 'She's my mother. It's not fair that you have her and not me!'

Ricky responded by joyfully hurling his teddies out of the cot. They thudded across the floor.

Grandma opened one eye. 'Oh, Ricky,' she murmured heavy with sleep. 'Not again.' She tried to ignore it this time. She hoped that he would get distracted by something else, but Ricky bounced up and down, rattling the bars of his cot and yelling to have his teddies back. She sighed and tried to look stern. 'This is the last time I pick up your teddies,' Grandma said, getting wearily to her feet. 'I'm not picking them up again, do you understand me,

Ricky?' and she scooped the teddies off the floor and dumped them back in the cot.

Ricky beamed at Chad as though to say, 'See what a good game this is?'

Chad scowled back. 'Horrid game. Silly game. You're silly!' he shouted.

But Ricky took it as a joke and laughed merrily. 'Play, play, play with me!' he gurgled without words, though Chad understood.

'I won't play with you. Why should I? I hate you,' sneered Chad and, to prove it, he leapt into Ricky's cot and flung all the teddies out again. 'There! She won't pick them up again. You'll have to do without them!'

Grandma heard the thud thud thud. From the corner of her eye, she saw them whizzing across the room. 'Gracious me, he is getting strong,' she muttered to herself, but then firmly closed her eyes saying, 'I warned you, Ricky. I told you I wouldn't get them again. You'll just have to wait,' and she dozed off.

Ricky chortled and bounced up and down in a frenzy. He pointed frantically at all his teddies. He wanted them picked up.

'Pick them up yourself!' snorted Chad, leaping out. 'I'm not your slave.'

But everything that Chad said or did, Ricky found funny and he just laughed or tried to copy.

Chad pressed his face up to the bars of the cot and looked into his half-brother's face. 'Eh! Hate you!' he jeered, sticking out his tongue rudely.

Ricky stuck out his tongue back and copied. 'Eh . . . eh . . . eh!'

'Silly boy,' said Chad.

Ricky laughed and pointed to his teddies. Then he sat back on his bottom and looked at Chad with huge brotherly love. 'Please.'

'You always wanted a brother, didn't you?' Chad heard the wormholers sighing in his ears. He looked into Ricky's sea-blue eyes. A stone rolled away from Chad's heart. He didn't know why. Something about the way Ricky looked at him which reminded Chad of how his mother used to look when she wanted something.

'Oh, all right!' Chad gave in. He sped round picking up all the teddies.

Ricky shook the bars with pleasure and made room for Chad who, with a leap, landed in the cot and arranged the toys round the sides. 'There you are!' he exclaimed, then sprang back on to the rocking horse.

'I love you, Chad,' Ricky's eyes said.

Lyn paused in the doorway, puzzled. The wooden horse was rocking violently.

Ricky didn't turn when his mother came in, but Chad fell off the horse in shock.

'Let's go. Come wormholing, Chad,' hummed the wormholers.

'That's my mother. My mother's here,' cried Chad. 'I wish . . . I wish . . . I hate her, I hate her. She left me!' and he sobbed with rage and misery. 'I wish I could . . .'

'Could what?' asked the wormholers. 'Go? Stay? Hate her? Love her? Do you want to stay? Is this where you belong?'

'Yes. No. Oh, I'll stay a while, just a while,' said Chad. He felt the cord which had bound them, running through his hands like sand. He climbed back on the rocking horse and rocked hard. He stared at his baby half-brother; stared into his limpid, blue eyes that seemed like open windows into his brain, into some previous creation – at the

120

end of one life and the beginning of another.

'Do you love him or hate him?' asked the wormholers.

'I hate him. I think. But . . .' he murmured thoughtfully, his anger dying down, 'I've always wanted a brother.'

Ricky thrust his arm through the cot bars and tried to touch Chad. 'Play with me!' he begged.

'Why is it Ricky sees me but my mother doesn't?' Chad asked the wormholers.

'He is young, close to the back time,' they murmured mysteriously. Ricky chuckled uproariously and threw a teddy at the prancing horse.

Grandma woke up and saw Lyn standing in the doorway. 'Hello, dear. Did you have a nice walk?'

'There's a school of whales close to the shore,' Lyn told her with excitement. 'I've been watching them. Everyone in the town has rushed down to see.' She went over to Ricky and picked him up. 'Hello, darling. I hope you had a bit of a sleep while I was away.' He didn't look as if he had. His eyes were bright, almost feverish, and his cheeks were flushed.

She turned to look at the rocking horse again, but it was still. She mused, briefly puzzled, but instantly forgot why when she glanced at the cot.

'Oh, look at Ricky! Look what he's done with his teddies. He's arranged them all round the cot. Isn't he clever! He's never done that before.'

'But that's impossible!' Grandma got shakily to her feet. 'Ricky threw them all out. I was tired of having to get up endlessly to put them back in the cot, so I left them.'

'You must have done it in your sleep!' laughed Lyn, going to pick up her baby. 'Why don't we all go down and show Ricky the whales. I love whales.'

Grandma marked her book and closed it, frowning at the mystery of the teddies. 'How did they get back in the cot?' she murmured. She saw just one by the rocking horse. She got to her feet to pick it up but, though her eye only left it for a second, when she looked again, it was gone.

'Hey, Chad, we're going to see the whales!' yelled Ricky. 'Come too! Come too!' and he bounced up and down so hard he nearly jumped out of Lyn's arms.

Chad hugged the teddy bear.

They pushed Ricky in his push-chair across the headland from where they could look down at the sea and the beach. Fifteen or so long grey shapes moved, slow as clouds, just below the calm unruffled surface of the ocean. People were gathering on the shore, their curiosity turning to anxious agitation.

'Oh no! Why do they do this?' Grandma gave a cry of dismay as she saw the whales heading for the shore. Everyone knew what would happen. If the whales beached themselves they would die. Some young men and women dragged out boats and began rowing out to meet the creatures, shouting and splashing in a desperate attempt to turn them back. Surfers got on their surfboards and raced into the waves yelling, 'Go back, go back!'

'They're turning! It's working!' Lyn clasped her hands with fearful joy. 'But look! There's one who won't turn back. Over there on the far side.'

One whale continued towards the shore, rolling on the incoming tide. By the time the boaters and the surfers and the swimmers and the people on the shore had realised, it was too late. The last great wave carried the huge sea beast inwards and deposited it on the land, before turning with the tide which ebbed back, back, back, exposing more and more of the glistening sands.

Lyn ran down with others, desperate to save the

whale. They rushed to prepare a line-up of buckets to splash its vast body in an attempt to keep it moist and alive.

When she reached the spot, the crowd around the beached whale was already two or three deep. Word had spread, and sightseers began arriving. People were poking and prodding at its vast body. A child begged to be lifted up to sit on its back. A youth fingered his knife, wondering if he could chop off a bit of its tail as a memento.

'We'll have to mount a guard until the next high tide,' shouted Lyn. 'Otherwise some idiots will try and take pieces of him away.'

There was a murmur of approval. An old fisherman began to build up a rota of people willing to stay, keeping the whale wet and watching out for souvenir hunters. Lyn said she would come and take a turn to guard the whale after she had put Ricky to bed. When she had satisfied herself that the whale would be protected for the moment, she, Grandma and Ricky hurried back home.

The black of the night hung like a prince's cloak, sparkling with jewels, somehow magical, as if it had enveloped the world with the toss of an arm.

'Why don't you let me go,' said Pete as Lyn prepared to go down to the shore and take her turn.

'Let's split it,' said Lyn. 'One of us has to stay with Ricky. Let me go first for a couple of hours, then you come.'

The next high tide would be at four o'clock in the morning. It was going to be a long night, but the helpers were eager. They built a fire with driftwood, a little way down the beach so as not to overheat the whale. Someone brought a catch of fish which they wrapped in newspaper and soaked in the salty sea. Then they buried it in the hot ashes of the fire to cook for their supper. The sparks spiralled upwards, brilliant orange. They reflected in the black eyes of the whale. And all the time, a steady line of helpers trudged to and fro to the edge of the ocean to fill buckets of water and heave them back to splash over the great creature.

When Lyn came down, she went over to the whale first before joining the others. She ran her hand along its marvellous body. She remembered its history, its ancient origins, its perfect design for its own habitat – and yet so vulnerable when out of it. She knelt by its head and looked into its eye. 'Why did you come?' she whispered. 'You're intelligent. Your brain is six times larger than ours. You have the knowledge of fifty million years of existence on this planet, so why, why did you keep on swimming into the shore when the others turned back? You must know it could mean death.'

The eye of the whale seemed to grow bigger and bigger so that it captured her reflection in its gaze – and suddenly she seemed to see Chad looking out at her. Her salt tears mingled with the seawater as she pressed her face against the creature's head. Then she raced across the gleaming sands, towards the surf breaking white in the moonlight. 'Chad!' she called out into the wind. 'I'm sorry I left you. I'm coming to see you soon. Don't forget me. Please don't forget me.'

Was it the warmth of the fire? A sudden breathlessness in the night which lulled the whale watchers into a sleepy reverie? Was it the incessant roll and thud of the waves breaking in mesmeric rhythm, or the distant harmonies of the whales whistling and calling out at sea which drugged their minds? No one really knew. When Pete came down to the shore, a long thin silver crack dividing night from day had opened up in the deep, dark sky. He stood for a moment on the rocks, looking down at the huddle of people round the embers of their fire. The incoming tide was creeping closer and closer up the shore, but there was still about three metres left to go.

He looked for Lyn. She wasn't near the fire. And where was the whale? He looked up and down, but the beach was desolate except for the sleeping watchers. Then he saw her. He felt a crunch of fear in his stomach. 'Lyn!' he yelled. 'Lyn!' He slithered and slid down to the shore and began running. She was lying spread-eagled on the sand just where the waves were now lapping at her feet.

His desperate cries awoke the other whale watchers. They struggled to their feet, rubbing their eyes, feeling a rush of guilt as they realised that they had slept while on duty. They looked around, bewildered at Pete racing across the sand.

'Lyn!' He bent over her. A wave dashed on to the shore and thrust itself forward till it swirled round her knees.

Lyn opened her eyes and smiled. 'Hello, Pete,' she murmured.

He clasped her under the armpits and dragged her

away as the next wave crashed and swept over her. 'What happened? What are you doing?' he cried, pulling her up into his arms. 'Are you ill? Are you hurt? You could have drowned. And where's the whale?'

The whale watchers were straggled across the beach, staring, puzzled. Lyn got to her knees and then her feet as gradually everyone moved in closer and closer. Wonderingly, they clustered together on the spot where the whale had lain. They looked out to sea, out to the horizon turning from grey to pink. Long, mournful notes mingled with the gulls, which swooped white, like the fountains spurting from the distant school of whales moving slowly out across the ocean.

'I must go to England and see Chad,' Lyn cried into the wind.

13
... AND ALL THAT MOVE IN THE WATERS

They inhale.
As the air enters the endless corridors of their bodies,
It gives off the sound of a reverberating bell.

Heathcote Williams

'What kind of place is this?' Sophie asked.

All around her was a quivering world of sound – a landscape of echoes. Her whole body was like a musical instrument, a sounding board which ricocheted with clicks and beeps and whistles and throbs and choruses of song. She heard and felt heart-vibrating frequencies: bass notes which seemed to grind out of the caverns of the deep and up through her feet; high-pitched notes which skimmed across the surface of her skin, strumming the hairs on her head.

Sophie reverberated with sound images and tried to see. 'Am I blind?' she asked wonderingly. 'All I see with my eyes are watery shades of pale blue deepening to darkest black, and shapes which move like great grey clouds, or pale flickerings like fireflies, or flocks of birds skimming like dappled shadows, or mysterious glimmering lights like distant stars. I can see but it is as if my ears are my eyes. I can tell shape and size. I know how near or how far, how narrow or how wide. I even know detail and texture, but I perceive all things by the sound they make and the vibrations I feel rather than by what I see.'

'We have our successor.' The message hummed through the soles of her feet.

'Professor?' Sophie turned to look. 'Where am I?'

'Always questions,' the voices rippled. 'That's why the professor likes you.'

'What place is this?' Even as the words fell from her mouth, Sophie realised she was talking easily. It was wonderful.

'You are home. You just need a bit of adapting. Then you'll be in your element. Are you pleased?'

'I don't understand. How do I know I'm home?'

'Home is the place you were designed for. Everything is designed for somewhere. The cactus for the desert, the whale for the ocean, the polar bear for the ice, the bird for the air and the worm for the ground. Can't you feel it? Can't you hear the world you are in? Professor Tlingit brought you here to the Dome, to your perfect environment. You are just what we need. You will have the power you wanted and you will also become our successor to Professor Tlingit. The professor has been wanting to self-change from this universe for some time now, to return to a multi-particle state.'

'I feel so free – and yet . . .' she paused wonderingly. 'I don't feel quite right here,' said Sophie. 'Are you sure this is where I should be?'

'Quite sure.'

'And what about my mum and dad and Chad and Natalie?' But even as she remembered them, she slid into forgetfulness in a new sound-space universe.

Far out in the other time-space, the anchor loosened once more. Chad and the wormholers swam with the whales.

'Where now?' asked Chad. He hugged Ricky's teddy to his chest and lay spread-eagled across the huge shining back of a great blue whale. The whale began to sing. Its notes seared through Chad's body and out again, threading messages along the communication channels which crisscrossed the ocean.

'What else did you come for?' asked the wormholers.

Gopher was waiting and whistling. He had been tagging along for quite some time. Catching the end of a line when they delved through another wormhole and always ready to snatch up a memento for his collection and toss it into his sack.

Every time Chad glimpsed his roly-poly body, he knew he should be remembering something.

Gopher saw Ricky's teddy bear. He whistled with envy and wanted it. He could see by the way Chad was holding it that he wouldn't let it out of his sight and Gopher knew he would have to watch and wait for a weak moment.

He sidled up to Chad and made friendly conversation. 'Where did you get that?' he asked, grabbing the cord just behind Chad.

'It's my brother's,' said Chad. He liked the sound of that: 'my brother's'.

'I'd like one of those for my collection.'

'You can't have it,' said Chad, tucking it tightly under his shirt.

'Hmmm,' snorted Gopher, tumbling away. He swung open his cosmic sack and snatched at particles of meteorites and bits of ancient spaceships. He came back again and again, fixing his eye on Ricky's teddy bear. 'Give me, give me, give me!' he pleaded.

'Where did we meet before?' asked Chad, his curiosity beginning to nag at him – as if he knew there was something important to remember, but he didn't know what.

Gopher plunged a tentacle into his sack and drew out a silver chain. It dangled, spinning so fiercely that its sparkle almost blinded Chad. 'Swap!' he shouted.

Chad shut his eyes then opened them fast. When it stopped spinning, he saw what was attached to the chain. The letter N.

'Heh, heh, heh!' chortled Gopher. 'N for Natalie, N for Natalie,' he repeated like a playground rhyme. 'I'll give you N for that,' and he prodded the bear.

'Natalie!' The name brought her image, large as

life, before Chad's eyes. 'Where did you get that? Where is she?' he exclaimed.

'Natalie!' sang the wormholers and a sudden tug of the cord took them diving down into the sea. Deep, deep, deeper. A hole opened up in the ocean floor and Chad and the wormholers plunged through.

In the hard metallic universe, somewhere within the structure of a rock, Chad saw the words scratched on stone: *Natalie is lost.*

'That's why I came,' Chad told the wormholers in a burst of memory. 'I came to find Natalie.'

'Natalie Lost is home,' chorused the wormholers. 'She's where she wanted to be.'

'Show me!' said Chad.

14
THE STREAM OF TIME

All laws are indifferent to time

Déjà vu. Been there. Seen this. Done that. All this has happened before.

This is what Natalie thought, as time for her continued in reverse. She felt like a piece of elastic, being pulled both ways between what she had once become and what she had been.

Her memory ran forwards and backwards as she lived that time again with her mother and father – her real, real father, not Chad's father.

'Now I know why I let go and came here,' breathed Natalie.

As always, there was the lake. It was the centre of

her forwards/ backwards motion. She saw her image in the water. Although she was now living her back-to-front life as though it were normal, she couldn't help a vague feeling that she was not where she should be. She couldn't explain it. She was living her life twice over. Everything that was happening, had happened before.

She had been at the lake before, many times, and the tangle of woods: brittle and crackly in the winter, bursting with growth in the summer and a treasure ground in late September, when the blackberries drew them like gold-diggers, with buckets and baskets to pick and pick until their fingers were purple and their arms criss-crossed with scratches.

They knew all those secret, meandering paths, its dips and its hollows – so good for playing hide-and-seek, and its circles of soft dappled grass where they would spread out their picnic on a red chequered cloth. Voices and laughter rang out among the trees.

Life wound itself backwards. Backwards, backwards. Happy, sad, sadder, saddest.

'I don't want to live that pain again,' she cried. But she had to.

She was in a graveyard. A small procession of

people wearing black or grey moved with bowed heads among the gravestones. She heard quiet murmurings and the sound of weeping. The wild grasses and flowers grew high and uncut, so that she had to peer at the mossy headstones to make out the names. There was the horror of the spot that was specially cleared, and the hole in the ground that was specially dug – deep in the rich red earth, wide enough to take a coffin. Shovels flung back the grasses and flowers which enveloped it. Red earth spewed outwards, raining down all around as slowly the coffin was revealed and hands with ropes were lifting it out. Borne high on shoulders, it was carried into the church. Natalie was with her mother walking silently, stiff with grief.

'I am the resurrection,' the vicar's voice had intoned, the words blurring as they echoed round the church. Natalie had an image of her father suspended between earth and sky as in pictures she'd seen of Jesus. With arms outstretched he soared through shafts of sunlight. But what did he do when he got to heaven? What would her father do? Would he just hang there – a bundle of dust mingling in sunlight? Or would he be reading and walking and listening to music and being a teacher. She couldn't imagine and her inability to picture what he would do made her distress worse. Then somehow, out of all the many biblical words which flowed monotonously from the vicar's mouth, suddenly something made sense: 'Behold I shew you a mystery; We shall not all sleep, but we shall all be changed, In a moment, in the twinkling of an eye, at the last trump: for the trumpet shall sound, and the dead shall be raised incorruptible, and we shall be changed.'

'Hey, Mum!' She had tugged her mother's sleeve fiercely. 'That's what Hindus believe too. You know, that people don't die, they just change and become something else,' and her mother had shushed her with distraught eyes and drawn her close in a crooked arm. Natalie had watched the millions of specks of dust floating in the shafts of sunlight pouring through the narrow arched windows of the church and wondered if that is how Dad would look.

There had been so many wasps that year, she remembered. They always made Natalie panicky. They had gone blackberrying in the woods and filled buckets and buckets. More had gone into Natalie's mouth than into her basket. But as they sat picnicking, the wasps came, disturbing their peace, sending Natalie into a frenzy. So they gave up trying to beat them off and decided to go home. It was her fault.

'It was all my fault,' Natalie was crying. It had happened in the past – and was about to happen all over again in this replay from the future.

'Come on, Natty. Let's get you out of here,' said her father kindly, as she dodged and squealed at every wasp. He and Mum stored the brimming buckets and baskets in the boot of the car.

'No, no!' begged Natalie the second time round. She hung back. 'Don't go.'

But there they were, climbing into the car. Mum in front, Natalie strapped in at the back. 'I can't stop it happening.'

The car bounced its way along the woodland track and out on to the main road – the long, winding, country road which would take them home.

'I know what's going to happen. I know!' Natalie had to live it all again: the wasp suddenly there in the car; her frantic screams as it swooped towards her; the stab of pain on her cheek. 'It's stung me! It's stung me!' she shrieked, flapping frantically.

'Don't turn round, Dad. Don't turn round,'

Natalie beseeched him, second time round.

But her father turned round. How could he not, at the sound of his child's pain?

'It was all my fault,' Natalie wept. *Bang*! Their faces spun, the car somersaulted. Faces and hands lifted them. Sirens of police cars and ambulances. Then there was oblivion. She stood by her father's body. Her mother nudged her gently. 'Say goodbye, Natty.'

She had to say goodbye. She kissed his cold white face.

Time ran backwards. His eyes opened. He smiled.

'It was worth all that pain. I would live it all again and again, to see my daddy come alive once more,' Natalie cried joyfully.

Less sad, happy, happier, happiest. 'I have my father back! Now I know why I'm here – and I never want to leave.'

Each day that she grew younger and younger, her worries fell away. The gentle joys of childhood dulled her memories of the future that was behind her instead of in front of her, and her past unfolded on and on.

'I love you, Daddy.' She was in his arms, holding his face close to hers.

'I love you too, Natty.'

Natalie laughed out loud. How long ago since she heard that silly nickname. She put her small hand into his, loving the feel of his huge palm enveloping hers. 'Swing me!' she begged. He swung her. She had done it all before and had been happy.

While she still had strength, she went back again and again to the same old tree in the woods. She built herself a den in its hollow and lined it with dry leaves. She loved the dark, earthy smell of growth and decay. It was as if this was her birthplace. When she learned against its huge body, she could hear the sap rising deep within like a slow song.

The surface of the lake was still as glass; the trees and sky a perfect mirror image. She watched through half-shut eyes as the sunlight wove itself in and out of the shadows.

There was a sudden churning. Ripples flowed crazily, first in one direction, then in another. The floating leaves went into a spin. A water bird flapped anxiously and, with high-pitched cries, made for the reeds near the shore. From the very centre of the vortex, a boy rose before her.

A voice was calling her name. 'Natalie!'

She knew the voice – and hated it. 'Go away!' she shouted. 'I hate you.'

'Let's go back now. You were lost, but now you are found. Let's go home!' Chad stared at the strange old child.

'I don't want to go with you!' she roared. 'I'm not lost. I'm here with my mother and father. I want to stay with them in the past time.'

'But what about your future?' Chad tried to reason with her. 'If you don't come back through the wormhole with me, you'll only have your past – and there's not much left of that – and you'll lose all your future. Come back with me, Nat! Together we can get home.'

'I want to stay with my dad,' she cried.

'But, Natalie, listen. You've had this life already. You're just repeating everything. Don't you realise, you're going back to being a baby and then you'll go into the pre-birth state – and there'll be no Dad, no Mum, no nothing. It will be like dying.'

Natalie screamed, 'Go away, you nasty boy. If I leave my dad it will mean living with you and I hate you. You hit me! And you always take my things.'

'Liar!' shrieked Chad indignantly. 'You're the one who took my hair gel.'

'It wasn't your hair gel, it was mine!'

'Did you hear that?' Chad shouted in an enraged voice. 'I told you she was a pain.'

Their angry voices echoed across the lake.

'Well, stay here then, you idiot. I don't want you in my life. Go back to being a tadpole. See if I care!'

The wormholers began to move on. 'It's crazy,' cried Chad, shaking with anger and confusion. 'How can I go home, if she doesn't come too?'

'Come on, come on!' urged the wormholers. 'We can feel the tremors. Look, a new wormhole is opening up. Another universe is being born. Quick. Let's go, let's go. There's nothing like being in on the birth of a new universe.'

'Natalie,' he called out one last time before he emerged out of the wormhole of Natalie's past, 'your father may be lost to you in the future, but what about your mother? She's been looking for you everywhere! What am I going to tell her?'

'Mum!' Natalie gave a sudden shriek of terror.

Then her father was there, scooping her up and laughing. 'There you are, you scallywag. Come on.

It's all right. Mum's over there!'

Her mother's face bent over her.

'Mum mum mum mum . . .' Natalie's words became a babble and her bed became a cot.

Chad felt the cord burning in his hands as he and the wormholers whooshed back out of the wormhole of Natalie's past and flared like a struck match into a newly formed universe.

'Look!' The wormholers broke up into a fine spray. Chad hung suspended: a fine, miniscule droplet. He was nothing but air and water, part of the bubble which was growing around him, shining and wobbly, it trembled with reflected rainbows, expanding outwards, on and on and on . . . mirroring in itself light and darkness; earth and water; creating its own sun and moon and stars; flaring with volcanic fire and liquid metal. But as it grew bigger and bigger, its shining sides strained with the effort.

'It's not going to make it,' cried the wormholers in a rush of murmured voices like fine rain. The glittering sides expanded out and ever outwards, growing thinner and thinner and thinner till – POP.

Chad and the wormholers fell in a cataract of collapsed universe.

'Wheeeee!' He could hear Gopher whistling as he skimmed after them, riding on the end of a comet's tail, his sack trailing behind like a fisherman's net, trawling for whatever came in its way.

'I like wormholing.' Chad was exhilarated. 'This is far better than school. Far better than being at home with Angie – and that dreadful girl Natalie.'

'Natalie . . . N . . . N . . . N . . .' Gopher leapt up beside Chad, twirling the silver chain and the letter N. 'I'll swap you this chain for the teddy bear!' he whined.

'Never, never, never!' yelled Chad, holding the bear to his chest. 'This is my brother's bear.' He felt the tug of the cord in his hands as the wormholers reformed back to a solid and plunged down into the ocean.

15
FORBIDDEN DREAMS

To exist, thought does not need any place or depend on any material thing

Descartes

Sophie glided along the canal to the regeneration suite. Her body was enclosed sleekly in a smooth grey skin so that her legs propelled her like a fish's tail through the clear, blue water. She could move with perfect control. She had no further memory of when she had ever sat in a wheelchair. She had no memory of where she came from. The only meaning was here in the Dome of Sound-Space Continuum.

The people she loved were her tutor, Professor Tlingit, her best friend, Lockhard, and her parent computer. Her body and mind had been completely redesigned and, so far as she knew, she had been in the Dome since her existence.

It was her regeneration day and, as usual, she was to have the full body and brain regeneration programme. This meant body maintenance: an organ check to see if heart, lungs, gills, kidneys or any other organ needed replacing and an artificial-additions check. Finally she would have an hour-long session in the brain capsule where she would receive an electrical booster to her brain cells.

There were only DMs – dolpho medics – in attendance as she entered the dark regeneration area. The only light came from their pale phosphorescent bodies. They moved silently round the suite, carrying out tests. The results were fed into the SH3 physician computer which printed out the diagnosis and prescription for treatment.

'Hello, Sophie. Happy Regeneration Day.' She was greeted by Roy, one of the DMs. 'Good to see you again? Any problems?'

'Not really,' answered Sophie. 'Though I'm glad I'm up for the brain booster. My front lobal memory hasn't felt quite up to scratch recently.'

'That's normal. It's a long span between one regeneration and another,' smiled Roy. 'We'll soon fix that. Enter capsule seventeen,' and he indicated a glassy, jelly-like tube into which she wriggled.

Sophie allowed herself to be connected to a series of electrodes which were linked to different parts of her brain. She liked this bit. Lying there in the darkness, her mind always felt more free than at any other time. Soft currents of electricity buzzed up and down her limbs, massaging her into total relaxation. Gentle slithers of sound calmed the membranes of her supersonic ears so that she was close to sleep.

Roy's smooth, grey, chuckly face peered in through the window at her. 'OK?' he asked in his clickety-click voice. 'Are you ready for the booster?'

Sophie managed a brave grin and nodded. The booster would be a charge of high energy straight into her brain. The pain was piercing, but as it lasted only three seconds, she'd barely have time to cry out before it would be over. 'Ready,' she said.

Roy vanished, taking his body light with him, plunging her into a coffin-like darkness. A high-pitched buzz told her that Roy had activated an energy source. It always started gently. First an orange light came on, then a series of purple lights. Sophie felt the wiry tentacles attached to her head beginning to throb. The charge was gradually increased, then her body jolted fiercely as she received the full blast. Fire seared into her brain. One, two, three. It should be over now. But it wasn't. The pain went on and on. Sophie began screaming.

A Dome night is never completely dark. A deep blue, not quite black, throbs with the sound of the Dome's vast oceanic generator.

Lying on her water bed in the rest bay, Sophie tried to understand what had happened to her. She had seen images. The sort of images that could only come through eyes or optical memory. She had seen faces in her mind, outlines and colours which she couldn't make out. It had never happened before. Dome people never saw pictures in their minds. Of all their senses, their eyes were the weakest. It was not her eyes which told her how big a space was or what was in it, but her ears creating echo pictures, telling her the dimensions of a room and what objects were in it. Her perceptions were received through her ears in sounds which throbbed or bounced off surfaces when she whistled, clicked and hummed.

Sophie tossed restlessly. 'Lockhard!'

'Mmm.'

'Something funny happened to me today in the brain booster.'

'What?' mumbled Lockhard. He was almost asleep.

'I don't know for sure. Something went wrong. They overcharged me. Perhaps it was a power fault – I don't know – but they nearly blew my brains. It was terrible. I was yelling to be let out, but those DMs didn't notice anything, the dumb idiots.'

'You should have pressed the alarm,' muttered Lockhard.

'I did, but it didn't work. I tell you, there was a fault somewhere. Something went wrong with my capsule. Roy and the others swore I was mistaken, because it didn't show up on the computer.'

'They're probably just protecting their own skins,' sighed Lockhard, more awake now. 'They know they would be discontinued for negligence if anything went wrong. You OK?' His water bed rocked as he rolled over, his voice expressing concern.

'Sort of.' Sophie opened and shut her eyes, testing them. What if she had no ears, would her eyes be enough to show her everything? She stared into the darkness wondering how much she should tell. 'I've got a bit of a headache . . . and . . .'

'And what?' asked Lockhard, wondering at Sophie's hesitation.

'While all that pain was going on, strange images came into my head. Pictures. Honestly, Lockhard, it was extraordinary. Have you ever seen pictures in your head?'

'Pictures?' Lockhard sounded wary. 'Do you mean echo pictures? What pitch were they? Were there any harmonies?'

Sophie suddenly decided to say no more. It had happened to Devi sometime back. She would have forgotten her friend had it not been for the overdose today. The effects were still there, for now suddenly she was overwhelmed with images of Devi. Her friend's face came into her mind: clear, as if she were right there. Sophie was remembering. Image memory instead of sound memory. That's what was different. Memory flooded back of Devi telling her she had seen pictures in her head after a brain boost. Devi hadn't wanted to report it to the chief programmer, but Sophie made her, because that was the rule.

You were supposed to report the slightest alteration in bodily or brain performance either in yourself or others.

'If only I'd known what they would do to you . . .' Sophie whispered to herself as more memories kept trickling into her brain.

The chief programmer had ordered total brain reprocessing. Sophie only saw her friend briefly afterwards. After TBR Devi was no longer Devi. She was no one, just an empty shell. Her face was blank like an unused disk; she recognised no one. Then Devi had gone. Reprogrammed and sent to another part of the Dome. Sophie forgot her because she wasn't allowed to remember.

'The pitch was muddled. As if the sound had got overlayed on to another frequency,' Sophie backtracked. 'They were more like feelings. Yes, that's what it was. Strange feelings. Oh, I expect it was nothing.' She paused and yawned. Then in a deliberately sleepy voice she drawled, 'Rest good, Lockhard.'

'Rest good, Sophie.'

The sounds of the night reduced to a low heartbeat.

The pictures kept coming. Sophie viewed her own mind. An incomprehensible jumble of images traipsed behind her eyes. She saw herself. Instead of swimming and diving or moving on two legs, she sat in a chair and wheeled herself around on solid ground. She saw faces and heard voices of people – alien people – different from her, yet the same. They walked upright. She felt she knew them, yet who were they?

There were eye pictures all round a wall. And colours – such glorious colours. The people were clothed in colours. It was amazing. She knew sound colours but didn't know of eye colours until now. One image in particular was etched clear; a great curve of green that went from one corner to another. Just dipping behind the green was a round, orange orb. The colours were so vibrant, she thought she could hear them humming. They were not the shades of grey of any landscape in her sound world.

She felt uneasy, yet excited. She felt on the brink of discovery, but she didn't know of what. She had seen pictures but did that make her mad, as the Dome always taught?

I have known something else before. The thought struck her like a blow. She began to sing softly,

'*Speed, bonnie boat, like a bird on the wing . . .*'

'Shut up, can't you,' complained Lockhard. 'I'm trying to sleep.'

The sonic brain scanner moved round the rest bay. A faint echosounder swept over the sleepers, probing for any forbidden brain activity such as illegal thoughts or picture-dreaming. Sophie had long ago acquired a technique to fool the machine. She lay still and created the rippled line of a single note in her head.

The sonic brain scanner moved on.

16
RANDOM SONG LINE

The naturalist knows that the bird of paradise is a crow, but he does not mistake either for the other

Donald Tovey

'Why is it wrong to see pictures in my head?'

Professor Tlingit sighed deeply and rolled over in the ocean. He had hoped the day would never come when Sophie asked that question.

Shoals of fish swam past him like a puff of bubbles, glistening briefly, then gone. He looked at the rod before him. This was his finest invention. At last, he had thought, he could see the time coming when he could pass on the rod and then demolecularise. He was weary of being chief tutor.

He was weary of being a solid. He had planned that Sophie should be his successor as Chief Tutor of the Dome, but then she had asked him the question he dreaded.

Today, as he watched Sophie poring over a calculation, he had sensed some disturbance. She was taking longer than usual and he knew it was an excuse. He had waited patiently. Finally, she completed the formula and looked up apprehensively but with complete trust. 'May I ask you a question?'

'Of course.' He had made himself smile. 'I just hope I can oblige you. Your questions have been quite complicated recently.'

Then it came. 'Why do I see pictures in my head?' He had shuddered, as if struck. She felt his dismay. 'I had to ask.' She shrugged apologetically. 'I'm sorry if I'm stepping out of line. I know it's breaking Dome rules, but why? I need to know why.'

The tutor stopped smiling. 'Mind pictures, did you say?'

'Yes,' said Sophie. 'Am I mad?'

He had tried to respond casually. 'What have you seen?' But inside him a deep chasm of despair was opening up.

'I have seen faces. Alien faces. I don't know them, not any of them, yet something makes me think I do. There was a space. I didn't hear it, I saw it. It was a small space, enclosed, with images on the walls and objects. I could see the objects – for sitting on and lying down on. I've never been to this place before, but – I knew what it was.' She had paused and looked half-afraid and half-embarrassed. 'Most of all, I saw myself. Not as I am here, but on land, moving on wheels. It was me. I saw with my eyes not my ears. Am I mad?'

'No, no, no!' He had tried to look reassuring. 'Not mad. Of course not.' But he knew some kind of floodgate had been opened and Sophie would insist on answers. Then there would be more questions and more answers. With genius the questioning never stops.

The dilemma hung heavily on him. He had always prided himself in giving answers and telling the truth. So how should he answer her? The Dome Guardians were unforgiving. Imagination, brain pictures, optical memory – such sensations were dangerous. They threatened the existence of the Dome and could not be allowed.

'Sophie,' he had begged. 'Don't move too fast. Let me lead you. I'll tell you which questions you should ask and I'll give you the right answers. But not too soon. What you have experienced is not important. It has no meaning. Probably one of your enhancer circuits is out of alignment. I'll arrange another appointment for you at the regeneration unit. Only what I teach you is important. If you think beyond that, you will just clutter your brain with rubbish.'

Sophie had listened tensely. He heard the anger reverberate through her body. He heard her thoughts angrily denouncing him. 'Don't patronise me. One of my enhancer circuits out of alignment, my foot! What do you take me for?'

'I'm not surprised you see pictures.' He had tried to soothe her. 'You clever ones often do.'

'Like Devi?' exclaimed Sophie.

'Yes. Like Devi,' he groaned softly.

'Why didn't you tell me before?' she asked.

Treason. How easily she had led him into treason. It could mean the downfall of both of them. 'I was afraid the Dome Guardians would get to hear and then you would be cancelled out as

Devi was,' he had said softly. The silence was vast.

He had altered his weight and drifted away into the ocean.

Funny that even though his powers had enabled him to function in any way he liked for as long as he liked, he had this weariness with existence. With each day that passed now, there was an increasing desire to hand over his powers and to disintegrate into a multi-particle state. The Dome was the core of all known universes and, because of that, the Dome Authority had been reluctant to let him go. His genius and skills had made him indispensable to the order of things. 'Before you demolecularise, you must find another genius worthy enough to take your place as Chief Tutor of the Dome.'

Somehow, despite all their advances in biotechnology and genetic engineering, they had not found anyone to compare with Professor Tlingit. They had experimented with all life forms, taking the best of each, whether it be mammal or insect, reptile or bird. They had been researching through space and time for his successor, but his genius was rare and unique and the Dome couldn't bring itself to let him go.

Then he had invented the supreme device – the sonic wormhole detector. It had taken him throughout time and space. It had brought Sophie to him and he knew that at last she was the answer. She would be his successor and release him from his solid state.

Not only was she a superb blend of biotechnology but she had the brain of a genius equal to his own. Even the Dome felt he had achieved enough. Professor Tlingit brought her to the Dome to train her as his successor, and he began to look forward to his molecular end.

She was adapted, reprogrammed, redesigned, re-educated; but they hadn't wanted to alter her brain too much for fear of losing the very thing which made her a genius, so he had known the risk was always there.

His instinct had been right though. Sophie was a genius. She had become his prize pupil, his protégée gradually earning complete access to the grand library where only the most privileged and trusted were allowed to study. Joyfully, he had watched her development. There is nothing more rewarding for a teacher than to see a pupil learn and thrive and even overtake the master. He had begun to see his end in sight – until this.

He increased his weight once more and drifted back down to stand before her, solid and implacable. 'Now is not the right time for this discussion. You are my chosen successor. The pictures are irrelevant, a blip in your genetic memory. Forget them.'

'What are my genetic origins?' Sophie challenged him again. She was suddenly aware of her insect-like limbs; her smooth, grey dolphin-like flesh; her body which could walk upright on dry ground and swim in the oceans. 'I'd like to know where I came from.'

'You are a whale, of course, with a few modifications.'

'What modifications? I need to know. I need to understand,' Sophie protested fiercely.

'Need. That was a universal word. Everything comes from need.' Sophie heard the grim change in the professor's voice. His face seemed to merge into grey as if he could not bear to face her. 'The only need is the need of the Dome. I need you because the Dome needs you,' he said. 'The session's over. Meanwhile, never tell anyone of your mind pictures or your dreams. You will certainly be certified mad if you do, and your genius would be lost to us. The penalty is reprogramming and there is no appeal.'

She was dismissed.

Sophie stared up at the pale stars which blinked feebly, as one by one they faded with the coming of the day. Once you ask the question, 'Why?' you have to know the answer. She lay right back in the ocean and tumbled over and over. If the professor wouldn't answer her, then she would find out for herself.

She swam to a far solitary shore. They called it the Edge. It was a rough, ancient place right on the outer edges of the boundary. It hadn't been developed like the other Dome shorelines, because it was too craggy for most Domers. Hardly anyone else went there because they found such land too uncomfortable. But that's why she liked it. She liked the ridges of water-moulded rocks: some liquid smooth, others like wind-whipped ripples which had suddenly petrified. They were jagged, razor-sharp under her feet, sending trickles of pain up through her body. Her thoughts and feelings were energised and focused. Her brain functioned quicker. She would work for hours on her calculations, her philosophical theories and the principles of aqua physics and cosmography.

There were few places where she walked rather than swam, but here was one of them. Even though it was painful, she loved the mystery and atmosphere of the ancient rocks and stones.

She made her way to one of her favourite caves, running her fingers along the water-scarred surface. Her fingertips paused on an indentation. She had often lingered here, relishing the feel of the strange pattern, wondering what it was. Perhaps it was an imprint of some fossilised creature. She had memorised a sonic impression of it and played it back to the organ computer. But the organ had told her, 'Random song line. No meaning.'

Today she felt the pattern again, pressing her face close to it, peering at it with feeble eyes. Seeing, rather than simply feeling the squiggles, gave them a different meaning; different because there was something familiar. Then it struck her with a shock. This was one of the pictures she had been seeing in her head.

I know the meaning of this, she said to herself. I know this. Once again, she ran her fingers over the surface. '*Natalie is lost.*' She spoke the words out loud without knowing why she spoke or what she spoke.

Excitedly, Sophie went to the grand library. She took a cubicle in front of the main frame organ computer and plugged herself in with headphones. She wasn't sure what she was listening for but, ever since her conversation with the professor, she had been trying to work out a way in which she could trick the organ into answering all her questions. It was a game. A matter of playing non-threatening melodic questions and then developing the tunes, penetrating further to extract the information she really wanted to hear.

She selected *Dictionary* and played the pattern of the squiggles in sound. She asked for the meaning of 'Natalie is lost'. She expected the organ to tell her 'not found' because the signs were after all just random squiggies, but she didn't expect it to say 'forbidden vocabulary'.

'What do you mean, "forbidden vocabulary"? Do they mean something?'

'Yes,' answered the computer.

'Do you know what they mean?'

'Not enabled,' it answered, and no matter how many different ways she played the tune, 'Natalie is lost', the organ steadfastly replied, 'Not enabled.'

'Right then. I'll have to try another way.' She called up her genetic record and played everything that she knew about herself. She heard back her various details. Her start-up date, her progress record, part replacement and servicing.

Having succeeded there, she then asked the organ for her genetic origins.

'Not enabled,' chanted the organ note monotonously.

'Why?' asked Sophie.

'Classified information under the Dome Secrets Act,' came the sung response.

She leaned back, frustrated, her fingers still trailing over the keyboard. She found herself improvising melodies and harmonies which would help her to think. She selected deep notes. Their pitches throbbed through her feet and shuddered through the vast chamber. She mingled the low notes with high ones, tumbling, ringing notes whose sounds overlapped. They rang in her ears and penetrated the cavities of her mind and she began to hum, her lips pressed together, the vibrations resonating like electric currents through the bones of her face into her teeth, forcing her mouth open.

Suddenly she burst into song:

Speed, bonnie boat, like a bird on the wing,
'Onwards,' the sailors cry.

She played on like one possessed, her voice ringing out and her excitement growing so that she thought she would explode. Something was happening. Soon she would learn more – she knew it.

She began to work out a strategy for getting the information she wanted. If she couldn't get her information legally, she would have to get it illegally. She would have to hack into the organ computer without its knowing that she was tricking it. Always ask simple questions. Devi had taught her that. Hacking is a step-by-step procedure. It was like crossing a raging river on stepping-stones: putting out a foot, finding a stone, testing it, then giving it your full weight before reaching out for the next stone.

She selected a stop labelled *Treble Voice*. She tapped sweetly, 'What am I?'

It was so easy, Sophie was shocked.

'Human,' sang the computer.

Sophie stared in disbelief. 'Human? That's not possible.' She played her question again. And again the answer was the same.

'Human.'

'What, completely? Am I not even half-whale?'

'Human origin one hundred per cent,' the computer confirmed. 'With some whale genetic input.'

Sophie felt turned inside out. 'I am not a whale.'

The professor had lied.

She wanted to explode, scream, run away, hurt someone, hurt herself. She had loved the professor. He was her parent, her teacher, her meaning. She had always trusted him completely. But now he had lied.

She fled from the library, back to her lagoon, back to the Edge. She plunged into its deep depths to swim and swim till she felt calmer.

She wept as she swam. 'I am not a whale.'

It didn't seem possible. Her culture was whale; her language was whale; everything she had been taught to believe was from whales. She didn't want to be anything else but whale. She certainly didn't want to be human. She shuddered at the thought. How could she belong to that fearful species, the human, which had so ravaged the cosmos?

Sophie rolled and dipped and dived and turned sad somersaults, singing a sad whale song. The fluting notes rose and fell, their mournful sounds wailing through the waters. After a while, the patterns of the whale song changed; their rhythms became short short long, short long, and odd utterances escaped from her throat. Suddenly, she was surging through the water, exhilarated, and as she leapt ten metres into the air, then plummeted down to the bottom of the ocean, she sang with all her heart.

> *Speed, bonnie boat, like a bird on the wing,*
> *'Onwards,' the sailors cry.*
> *Carry the lad that's born to be king*
> *Over the sea to Skye.*

17
MAKING CONTACT

Music is a process in time

Donald Francis Tovey

'Did you hear that? Did you?' Chad asked the wormholers.

Vibrations trilled up through the sea-bed, reverberated along ancient oceanic tracks and soared upwards into the air, ricocheting against everything which fell in its path. Chad felt the sound run over his body like fingers strumming a guitar. It made his skin tingle and his hair rise up on his arms and on the back of his neck.

'I think I know that song from somewhere,' exclaimed Chad.

169

'It could have come from any place and any time. Sound travels forever, from one universe to another,' the wormholers told him.

'I want to follow its track,' cried Chad, turning in the direction of the singing. He tugged at the cord and led the way, worming into rock and cave, into organisms and microbes, into water and gas, into air and light. The wormholers followed, Gopher tagging along at the rear, whistling away regardless.

Then, as suddenly as they had heard it, the sound ceased.

It was not that there was a silence. There is no silence in the oceans. There was just the cessation of the song – except for its reverberations, carrying on and on, as it would for ever: transversing the universes, mingling and transposing itself into endless harmonies.

Chad listened intently. 'Shut up, Gopher, would you!' he commanded, as Gopher's whistling continued nonchalantly.

A group of dolphins streaked by, clicking and chuckling. Chad called out to them. 'Did you hear the song? Where did it come from?'

They encircled him playfully, nudging and tickling

him. 'From somewhere, everywhere, nowhere. It doesn't matter to us. It was human anyway.'

'Human!' Chad let go the cord which bound him to the wormholers. He dived among the smooth, grey, undulating bodies. 'That's me! I remember now. I'm human. Can't you take me to them?'

'Take the cord! Hold on to the cord or we'll lose you,' warned the wormholers.

But it was too late. It was the moment Gopher had been waiting for. He hurtled among the dolphins, scattering them.

'The teddy, the teddy, give me the teddy.' Gopher's tentacles enveloped Chad.

Chad struggled, beating him off. He tried to grab back the cord as the wormholers soared upwards into the firmament. For a moment, he hung on, but a tentacle thrust inside his shirt and closed round the bear.

'Oh no, no! Don't take it!' cried Chad, using both hands to fight off the tentacles which entangled him. He and Gopher went tumbling over and over, twisting and writhing. They plunged through space, entwined together, spinning and twirling among the scattered debris of exploding stars.

Chad's cry of dismay ran rivulets along the ocean beds, causing schools of fish to swerve and change course and whales to come shooting to the surface with alarm.

'Why did he let go?' he could hear the wormholers chorusing as they coiled away like steam rising from the damp earth.

'Heh, heh, heh!' Gopher laughed and stuffed Chad and the teddy into his cosmic sack.

Chad raged helplessly, kicking and yelling. 'Let me out, you blithering idiot!'

'Give me teddy!' yelled Gopher.

'Never!' shouted Chad, clutching it to him.

He was immediately sucked into an orbit, rotating in a rainstorm of Biros and a buffeting of trainers and wellies. He curled up into a ball, sheltering his head from the whirling objects of Gopher's collection. He could hear sounds; grunts, whistles, clicks, hisses and sighs, as though they too had been collected. There were voices using hundreds of different languages; they chatted and laughed, and called and clamoured, and whined and questioned. Occasionally he thought he understood; 'Where did I put my glasses,' or 'I'm sure I left my jacket on this peg,' or 'Mummy! Have you seen my school bag?' or 'How is it things disappear in this house?'

But a particular sound caught his ear: a stammering, open-throated grunting . . . eh . . . eh . . . eh . . . and the song: '*Speed, bonnie boat . . .*'

'Sophie?' Chad stopped yelling. 'Sophie, are you here?' He peered out from beneath the crook of his arms.

And then he saw it. First the spokes, then the wheel, then a computer with its screen still flickering – and then the whole chair. Sophie's wheelchair.

'Sophie!'

Still holding on to the bear, Chad grabbed the arms of the wheelchair and hauled himself into the seat. For a while, he rotated in a daze, too confused to shape any real thought or understanding of where he was. He stared at the screen and, slowly, his memory flickered into life.

Automatically, he reached into his pocket for Professor Tlingit's calling card and slotted it in.

18
DREADFUL ORIGINS

Distinct species are not a fact of nature, but of language

Bertrand Russell discussing Darwin

'Sophie!'

'What?' Sophie tried to sound sleepy.

'Are you still seeing pictures in your head?'

Sophie was silent for a brief second. She hated to lie to Lockhard. 'No,' she lied.

'I wouldn't report you, Sophie. You know that. You're my best friend.'

Sophie was silent. Would he still want to be her friend if he knew what she really was? If he found out that she was human? She could hardly accept the horrible truth about herself.

Sophie had asked the organ computer for the name of her original, genetic parents. It gave her the answer. 'Original human birth David and Carol Walcott, 1984, Earth calculation. Later alterations and reprocessing by Professor Tlingit, MAM x GEN.'

She had listened in horror to a soundtrack which had played her past back to her. The sounds were so multi-layered, so dense, so high and low, so deep and wide that she saw exactly how she had been in a previous life. At first she could only take in a little at a time, having to rush away to find solace in the ocean; to swim up and down and dive to the very depths to calm her stricken soul as she realised what she was and from where she had come.

After a while she became calmer and was able to try and comprehend what she was learning. Not all of it made sense. If she was her parent's child then she seemed different from them. If she was human, she was differently powered. They moved only on land and on their two feet, whereas she only seemed to move on wheels in a sitting position. Why?

She had asked the computer, 'What was the language of the Walcotts?'

The computer replied, 'English.' She plugged in the translator disk and had instant access to meaning.

Natalie is lost. She brought the scratched patterns up on to the screen, and realised they were words which she had to peer at through her weak eyes.

'Natalie is human and Natalie is lost!' She remembered Natalie had been her friend before Lockhard, even before Devi.

Responding to Lockhard's warm friendship reaching her through the darkness, she said softly, 'You are my friend too, Lockhard. I'm sorry if I've been a bit withdrawn lately. I've been struggling with a rather difficult problem.'

The sonic brain scanner came by. It stopped a little longer in front of Sophie. She invoked the steady white line but was filled with anxiety that the scanner had detected some forbidden brain activity.

The scanner moved on. Sophie longed to tell Lockhard that she had made a decision. But she didn't dare. She wouldn't risk trusting anyone, not now, not even Lockhard, because Lockhard was pure whale. She had looked him up. Anyway, Lockhard was loyal. Loyal to the safe haven. He had never once needed reprogramming and Sophie knew that loyalty to the Dome went beyond friendship.

Now that she knew she was human, she longed to find more humans. Her curiosity to know drove her on and on, hacking through the organ computer, asking questions, going up one blind alley after another, but persevering, till finally, as she gained more knowledge, came the certainty that she must find a way of leaving the Dome to see for herself. There was no one she could trust. If the professor had lied to her once, he could lie again.

Hour after hour she sat in front of the organ computer, playing through the intricate instructions until she hacked her way into its inmost secrets.

Then, yesterday, something extraordinary had happened. She wished she could tell Lockhard, but she couldn't risk it. Only yesterday, she had been sitting before the organ computer when she picked up an unexpected signal coming via Uninet, the computer system which linked one universe to another. It was a strange, crackly signal, which broke up a few times. Then she heard it received and acknowledged. 'Beep beep bop beep beep bop bip.' It was then that Sophie realised she had accidentally tuned in to Professor Tlingit's personal line. She knew she shouldn't be listening, but she felt compelled to because she felt she had heard that signal before. 'Beep beep bop beep beep bop bip.'

'Professor, is that you? It's me, Chad!' The voice which crackled across the channel struck such a powerful cord of memory in her that tears sprang like a fountain from her eyes.

'Chad?' Sophie had been stunned. She knew the voice . . . perhaps the name . . . alien but familiar.

The professor answered. 'Chad! Good heavens, boy. I thought you had returned home. Still here, are you?'

'What do you mean, still here?' Chad had exclaimed, his voice distorted with annoyance. 'It's all your fault, I'm here. I followed you. Remember? You came to my house. You were supposed to be helping me to find Natalie but you went off back down a wormhole. Luckily, you left that rod thing behind. Sophie worked it out and we were able to follow you. But she got kidnapped by this creature. Now he's got me – and all that's left of Sophie is her chair. What shall I do? Help me! Please help me!'

'He said my name. This Chad knows me!' Sophie had gasped with amazement. Her brain had worked at top speed as she listened to their exchange. 'Chad? Who's Chad?' She had brought up a parallel score window and fed in Chad's voice pattern. She asked the computer for a fact file.

'Chad is a human,' the computer informed her.

Excitedly, Sophie drew more and more information out of the computer while still listening in to the conversation between Chad and the professor. It was almost too much to bear. 'Chad was your friend and neighbour at home,' said the computer.

'Home? Aren't I home here? Where is home?'

She heard Chad say her name again. 'Tell me where Sophie is. I must get to her. She can't function without her wheelchair. She must be in misery.'

'Stop blathering, silly boy!' snapped Professor Tlingit impatiently. 'Sophie is truly happy. Perfect happiness is to be where you are designed for. She's in her proper world now. She doesn't need the wheelchair any more. Gopher can keep it. As for you, you were in your proper place before and that's where you should return. Fortunately, you brought the rod with you – my cosmic wormhole detector which Gopher has given back to me. That's about the only sensible thing you've done since we met and even that, I suspect, was Sophie's idea. Without it, I wouldn't have been able to find your re-entry point. I'll see you and that other one safely back.'

'What other one?' demanded Chad.

'Your sister Natalie. Isn't that where the problem started?'

Natalie, Chad, Sophie. They were linked. Probably they were all human. Gradually, Sophie had begun to understand that somehow her past and her identity were tied in with them. *Natalie is lost.* Perhaps they were all lost.

She heard Chad say the word again. 'Natalie!' He paused. 'You can keep Natalie, but I'm not going back without Sophie.'

'Silly boy!' snorted the professor. 'Sophie doesn't want to go back. She's in her element here.'

'I don't believe you,' yelled Chad, angrily. 'Please let me speak to her.'

'That would be useless. She wouldn't know you. Wouldn't even be able to understand you.'

'I do, I do! I would be able to understand,' Sophie whispered over and over to herself.

'I assure you, she doesn't want to go back,' insisted the professor. 'She wanted power and freedom, and that's what she's got here. Now listen to me and try and obey. Keep my card slotted in so that we stay in touch. I'm coming to find you,' and he had switched himself off.

'Sophie!' Lockhard's voice broke into her thoughts again. 'Are you happy?' He was so finely tuned, he had picked up her anxiety vibes. 'I wish you would discuss your problem with me.'

'Dear Lockhard. Dear, dear Lockhard. Don't worry. It's nothing. Honestly. We'll talk in the morning.'

Finally, the ripples around Lockhard's water bed were still and he slept.

But Sophie didn't sleep. She waited, listening in ultrasound. All her senses alert. Because Chad had kept the channel open between him and the professor, Sophie too could tune in. She knew she must follow the professor. She could never accept her state until she had seen for herself who she was before and where she had come from.

'Beep beep bop beep beep bop bip.' It was so sharp inside her head, she wondered if Lockhard had heard it too. But there was no movement at all from him.

'Beep beep bop beep beep bop bip.' She tipped herself out of her water bed, all her telepathic senses on super-alert. The professor was on the move. He was going to meet this Chad. She would follow.

She glided out of the rest bay. The receptor lobe in her brain tracked the professor as he moved across the main zone area. She followed him down inland freeways, her grey limbs gleaming silvery in the darkness as she skimmed along a runway of short sonic blips. When the blips became longer and high-pitched, she knew she had entered the forbidden outer boundary.

Suddenly, she was sure she knew where the professor was headed.

Sophie had once found the file which revealed the exits out of the Dome. It had taken her weeks of hacking; devising innocent questions, entering a path, then double-backing in order to cover her tracks. Discovery would have meant instant brain reprocessing, so she had had to hold back her impatience. Slowly, slowly, burying each step in a flurry of calculations and mathematical formulas, she began to pinpoint the location of every outlet from the Dome. It was by accident that she stumbled on the blue hole. She thought she had made an error in calculation, for the computer kept bringing up a location Sophie had thought was an ancient defunct volcano on the bottom of the lagoon. She knew it was an artifical lagoon, created hundreds of years before, for mining and extracting mineral deposits. But when her calculations pinpointed that spot for the third time, she had to accept that the rock floor was a disguise for an exit hole.

She was halfway across the outer boundary, when the alarm went off. Sirens wailed and a Dome voice urgently warned, 'Exit alert. Exit alert! Unauthorised entry into outer boundary.'

Sophie stopped, confused. Who had set off the warning? She had been so careful. It must have been Lockhard. Best friend, she thought sadly, just as she had been Devi's best friend.

There was no going back now. She knew that. To go back was to face brain cleansing and be altered for ever. She must carry on. It was her only chance to learn the truth – even if it meant extinction.

Her calculation of the route had been perfect. Just as she had deduced, the unmarked passage opened before her. It would lead to the lagoon.

Alarm sirens shrieked louder, but the beeping signal between Chad and the professor still came through. She proceeded. The footing was difficult, unsuited to her design. She stumbled and fell, carried on, then fell again, so hard that her ankle revolved round the wrong way and one of her fins was crushed beneath her.

The alarms were closer, louder than ever. They were trying to incapacitate her brain. Powerful beams of sonic light sprayed around her. She was on her knees, slithering and crawling in any way that she could. Then a voice called out, 'Sophie! Wait for me!'

It was Lockhard. She saw him stumbling behind her. Sophie paused. She heard a distant throbbing like a vast machine. The Dome Guardians were coming.

'Go back, Lockhard. We aren't friends any more. You reported me, didn't you?'

'No, Sophie, it wasn't me. I swear. I didn't report you. Please wait. I want to come too.'

Her brain reeled with confusion. If Lockhard hadn't reported her, who had?

'Please, Sophie!' Lockhard wept. 'Don't do this. Don't go into the outer boundary. I don't want to lose you. There's still time to go back. We'll sort out your troubles, whatever they are.'

'Go away, Lockhard. I'm a human, don't you realise? I'm human, human! I would always disgust you. We can never be friends now.'

The sonic beams struck the deep black waters of the lagoon ahead. She reached the edge and looked down in terror. Steep rock sheered around it like the insides of a bowl. So smooth that she doubted anything could get out once it fell in.

She hesitated, but only for a moment, then toppled over. She was falling into space; she was falling through the darkest night. Down, down, she fell like a star, plummeting through the heavens. She thought her fall would never end.

She made no splash as her body hit the surface. Her entry into the water was like a hand parting a curtain of silk: cool, soft, smooth. She continued her descent towards the ocean floor.

The tips of her fingers and toes hummed. She had heard another sound somewhere beneath her. Her eyes got larger, expanding with the light which glimmered from fish as small as glow-worms. She heard a rumbling, distant vibration and calculated that it came from at least eight hundred kilometres away. She followed the sound path, down, down. She had never before swum to the Dome floor but, suddenly, she could tell from the soft coils of sediment swirling with the current that she had reached the bottom.

The water around her chorused with the sound. It was whale song. She knew it. The sound was coming from beneath her, from beneath the Dome floor. The bones in her feet were zinging with the energy, making her blood race through her body. Her fingers scrabbled through the sediment, sending up clouds of brown matter as she searched desperately for the source of the sound.

The grip of a vortex took her by surprise. It tugged her fiercely into a current, dragging her down, deeper and deeper, spiralling out of control.

No. Too soon. I'm not ready to leave! she thought, panic-stricken. She struggled, frantically beeping in an effort to find something to stop her being sucked down. Her sonic clickings picked up a rock face; she heard its craggy, volcanic surface. She stretched out a hand and clawed a grip on it. Her descent was halted, momentarily. Her hands hung on to the rock while her legs still trailed in the current. Slowly, slowly, she hauled herself closer to the rock, clicking her teeth to tell her what other features she could detect to save her. Just above, she heard the contours hollowing out into a small cave. She tried to reach upwards for it, but the strength of the current was too strong, and she felt herself being drawn away.

Suddenly a hand reached down and grabbed her wrist. She felt herself hauled up and pulled into the safety of the cave.

'Lockhard!'

'I couldn't let you leave me. I told you. I'm your friend. Wherever you go, I go.'

'Oh, Lockhard!' Sophie wept with shame. Shame that she could ever have doubted Lockhard's loyalty to her.

'Return to the Dome,' pleaded Lockhard. 'The professor will understand. He'll save you from being brain cleansed. Please, Sophie. Don't leave me.'

In the depths of her brain, Sophie heard the signal, 'Beep beep bop beep beep bop bip.' She heard the blue hole but now she knew it was a wormhole which led, not just out of the Dome, but out of the universe.

She listened to the sound it made. It was so different as to be terrifying. The sound echoed on and on without interruption, as though there was no end to the depth of the hole. Rising and falling and dwindling away . . . over and over again. Above the roar she could hear strange screechings. High mournful notes called out against the wind. Shivers of memory rippled through her brain – memories from outside the Dome. She knew she must go through.

'Lockhard. I must.'

They stared at each other. He bent forward till his face touched hers. They rubbed noses with loving affection and arched their heads, caressing and nuzzling into their smooth broad necks.

'I must, Lockhard,' she repeated softly.

'Yes, I know now. You must,' he said and, suddenly clasping her in his arms, he leapt from the cave into the abyss.

19
THE THING IN ITSELF

After a long winter of some centuries ...
Radhakrishna

A stretch of yellow sand; a thin line of earth between sea and sky. In the distance, a huge boulder – egg-shaped, like the beginning of life. It looked rooted into the earth, so still and solid and immovable. Yet its presence seemed to summon her before it.

Sophie tried to walk but her limbs were not enabled. She stumbled and rolled. Time ceased. Sleeping or waking, there was no difference.

'I need to speak to you,' she murmured as if to the boulder.

Immediately, she went into motion – not walking,

swimming or flying, but moving as the tides move, ebbing and flowing, till she found herself in its presence. She bowed her head and waited.

'Why?' she asked. 'Why did you lie to me?'

There was a great pause. Wormholes flickered and died.

'I needed you. You came from a world which was ravaged by a fearful plague called humans.'

'Like me,' said Sophie bitterly.

'Yes,' said the professor. 'But it is the uncertainty principle again. Like you in the whole, but not in the particular. For millions of years we had been at one with our environment, until they came. We were perfectly designed to fit in with the ecosystem, until they came. We interacted with other species, keeping perfect balance and harmony. We believed in the contentment of having enough, until they came – these humans.

'This new mammal was greedy, dirty and totally selfish. It was never satisfied; it always wanted more. It thought the world was theirs for the taking. It was infinitely clever and infinitely stupid – the worst combination. It even destroyed its own habitat because it could not work for the good of the whole.

It was dominated by the uncertainty principle – of particles and genes being obsessed with their own particular. So not only did they wipe out millions of species of all kinds of living things, but they killed each other too.

'Then began the holocaust of the oceans. We were about to be annihilated. We had to save ourselves. There were other particulars, like you, among the humans. They tried to do something but they were too few.

'A few generations after you, most of the planet was laid waste by these humans through pollution, deforestation and war. The ice caps melted; huge areas of land disappeared under water. What was left was barely able to sustain itself. Most of the world's species became extinct. We had to fight back. We took what knowledge we could of human technology. We interacted, species with species, to survive. We were able to adapt ourselves, genetically changing; some of us to have human or insect characteristics as well as whale. We developed our own technologies, seeking to explore the time-space universes to escape. We learned how to live forever.

'I discovered wormholes and led my species to a

new time-space zone where we created this safe haven – the Dome – our own universe. We suspended time-space. We banned inherited mind pictures because it would affect our security. Dreams are the storehouse of our memories. But dreams cause revolution. We couldn't allow that in the safe haven.'

'And what about me?' asked Sophie. 'How could you bear to have me here?'

'My dear!' The professor sounded suddenly desperate. 'You are the best of what humans were and the best of the whale. But don't seek to return to the world of humans. Don't find even the smallest desire to go back. For if you do, you will suffer in the dying of the world. Here you have all the power you never had before. If you leave the Dome, you will return to helplessness. I wanted you to be my heir. You, human though you are, were the best I could find in the universe. Better even than whales. You can't go back, Sophie!' The professor's voice echoed with grief. 'You are my heir, my successor. Without you, I am doomed to live on and on. Please, Sophie. How can you want to go back to a place where you have so little power? Here you would have all the power you ever wanted.'

Now Sophie understood who had betrayed her. 'I never wanted that kind of power, professor,' whispered Sophie. 'I want the power to be where I belong.'

Chad bent over Sophie. She was so still. He pressed his cheek to hers. Was she alive? Her skin was cold but he felt her shoulders shudder slightly. He loosened his hold on her.

'I heard you singing,' he whispered.

Sophie's hand rose, wavered around and fell again. Strange sounds squawked from her throat.

'I think you'll need this.' He heaved her up into her wheelchair. Sophie leaned forward towards her computer screen. Chad strapped the control stick to her head. Very slowly she tapped out the words. 'Hi, Chad.'

'You OK?' he asked.

'A-OK.' She held up both hands and wriggled her fingers then was still again, as still as before. He looked into her face and her eyes.

He shook his head, amazed. Her head was firm, her face relaxed. Her eyes glimmered. 'What do we do now, boss?' he asked.

'Find Natalie?' she asked.

'It's all right, Gopher collected her,' said Chad. 'He got her back with my teddy bear,' he added with disgust.

A baby rolled and chortled, clutching the teddy bear. Lolloping around nearby, Gopher whistled uproariously. 'Give me back the teddy bear. It's mine!' he chanted, twirling the silver N on the end of a chain. 'Swap you, swap you!'

Natalie's eyes fixed on the glittering letter of her name as Gopher dangled it lower and lower over her face. She dropped the teddy bear and reached up with demanding fingers. 'Mine!' she declared, pulling the chain down over her head.

'Mine!' shouted Gopher triumphantly, snatching away the teddy bear and dropping it into his sack.

'No, it's not, it's mine!' protested Chad, trying to grab it, but too late!

Sophie opened her mouth, tossed her head back and burst into song again.

Speed, bonnie boat, like a bird on the wing,
'Onwards,' the sailors cry.

20
RETURN TO BELONGING

The eye is worthless when separated from the body

Hegel

'Chad?' Angie stood in the doorway of his bedroom and looked perplexed. 'Good grief!' she breathed with annoyance. It was as if it had been hit by a tornado. What with Natalie leaving the bathroom in a mess and now Chad's bedroom in such a tip, she felt drained and defeated. She tried so hard to be a good mother. Trying to keep the house tidy; trying to make everyone happy; trying to keep the peace. But sometimes she wondered why she bothered. No one else seemed to care.

Suddenly the house seemed terribly empty. She

felt a strange feeling of unease. It wasn't natural. One minute Chad and Natalie had been going for each other hammer and tongs and the next minute the house was as silent as the grave. Where were they? She stared at the empty floor. There was something different. It looked as if Chad had been rearranging his furniture. 'Where the dickens is the carpet?' She stared at the bare boards stretching away into infinity, the cracks between them, dark and deep as chasms. She fancied one could fall through and disappear for ever. The thought made her feel dizzy.

The phone rang. It startled her, as if for a moment she had fallen asleep. She hurried downstairs and snatched it up. 'Oh, Amy! Hello, it's you. No, Natalie isn't here for the moment. I take it she's not with you. Yes, she was washing her hair. It must still be wet. I don't quite know where she is. I sent Chad over to Sophie's, perhaps she's turned up there. It was her turn. Yes, I'll get her to ring you. Oh, wait a moment, I think they're back. I can hear them.'

Voices came from upstairs, quarrelling voices which suddenly rang through the house.

'Why did you give him the teddy?'

'I swapped it for my chain.'

'How dare you, you blithering idiot. That teddy was mine!'

'No, it wasn't, dummy! He gave it me.'

'It wasn't his to give. It was mine.'

'I don't care. He gave it me so it was mine and I swapped it. I could if I wanted to. I didn't want a silly teddy anyway. I'm not a baby!'

The phone rang again. Angie snatched it up. 'Carol? Oh, Carol, I'm so sorry Natalie let you down. It was her turn to entertain Sophie. I don't know where she got to. Did Chad turn up? He did? What! He what?' Angie's exclamation cut through the air like an arrow. She listened, mouth open but speechless. Chad's father opened his study door and looked out. 'Everything all right, dear?' he asked blearily.

Angie slammed down the phone and rushed to the front door. 'That was Carol! First Chad makes off with Sophie without telling anyone, then he gets her, wheelchair and all, to the top of the stairs and leaves her stranded. Can you beat that? You're going to have to have words with that son of yours. I'm going round to give Carol a hand.'

The radio was on. Someone had chosen a record. It

was a scratchy old-time song. It crackled eerily through the house.

Speed, bonnie boat, like a bird on the wing . . .

Carol and Angie looked up the stairs. Sophie was in her wheelchair on the top landing, swaying gently to the music, grunting softly as if she was trying to sing with it.

'Come and see something else,' whispered Carol. She led Angie up the stairs till they could see Sophie's computer screen. The words flickered green and bold. 'I am a human being.'

When the song ended, the announcer said, 'Here is a news bulletin. A whale was stranded on the east coast last night. The RSPCA and animal lovers tried to guide it out to sea on the evening tide, but it beached itself again a little lower down the coast. A spokesperson said, "Once a whale decides on a direction, even if it's wrong, it is very difficult to make it change its mind. This whale seems determined to stay here, even though it means it will die. A further attempt will be made at the next high tide."'

Briefly, Sophie's jerking body was stilled. A single tear slid down her cheek. Then she leaned forward and tapped out the word, 'Lockhard'.

A universe burst into life, flickered, burned brightly, then died.

> *Will they ever come to me, ever again,*
> *The long, long dances,*
> *On through the dark till the dim stars wane?*
> *Shall I feel the dew in my throat, and the stream*
> *Of wind in my hair? Shall our white feet gleam*
> *In the dim expanses?*

Euripides

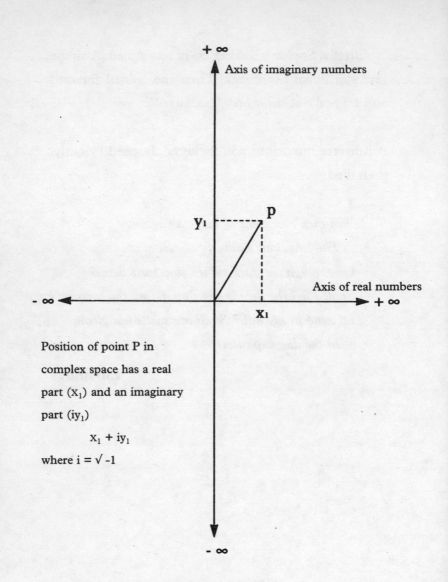

+ ∞

Axis of imaginary numbers

y_1 ------- **p**

Axis of real numbers

- ∞ ◄──────────────►+ ∞

x_1

Position of point P in
complex space has a real
part (x_1) and an imaginary
part (iy_1)

$$x_1 + iy_1$$

where $i = \sqrt{-1}$

- ∞

The number you have dialled is imaginary.
Please multiply by i and dial again.